for
EAVAN
my love

*Remember that light and shadow never stand still.*

CONSTABLE

# PART ONE

# Chapter One

Bannister woke early on his forty-sixth birthday and wondered if anyone had sent him a card. It seemed unlikely; his mother was too old to remember, his sister too busy to bother. It would be a difficult day. Staring at the ceiling he had a premonition of bitterness. A damp spot, shaped like a long, bruised finger, pointed and threatened and accused above his head. All that winter he had watched it grow more menacing as he patiently shook plaster from the unchanged sheets. A complaint to the concierge had met with a demand for long overdue rent. This had not surprised him. He was used to cheap rooms, to suspicion and hostility. Forty-six, he thought, trying to remember a time when birthdays had been happy. It was not easy. Once, in Paris, he had made slow love with a satisfaction that was entirely new but the birthday joy had vanished when, half-dressed, watching her dressing, he had paid for his pleasure with a crumpled wad of notes. I never had candles, he thought mournfully, or a cake. His childhood was a lost world of restrospective disappointment. On the street outside the Rif women were going towards the market. He could hear them shouting abuse at each other and belabouring the mules. A cart went by, its wheels creaking and a dog barked with an insistence that reminded Bannister of a debt-collector hammering on the door. He remembered the stuffy room in Paris, the small window, the big bed, her clothes thrown in a casual bundle near the fireplace, the money on the table. There had been a picture tacked to one of the walls, a cheap Madonna, gaudy and pious. "She keeps me company," the girl had said, as she pulled on a stocking and laughed as if hoping to shock him. He had not said anything. Watching her dress he had wanted to have her again but his wallet was

almost empty. His allowance had been due in six more days. It was always a little too late.

The bed creaked loudly as he shifted his weight. The damp stain seemed to have grown bigger. A time for caution, his horoscope had read, affairs of the heart could be deceptive. The end of the month brings financial improvement. Write overdue letters and settle domestic affairs. He lighted a cigarette and watched the smoke coil aimlessly upwards. It reminded him of incense in the dark, back parlour, the medium's frightening voice and the sweet, heavy smell. It was peculiar that he should remember that and the old and pointless horoscope for a month that was like any month except for a moment of love. Loose tobacco from the cigarette was bitter on his tongue. He spat it on to the dusty tiles and coughed. His throat felt sore and dry but he noticed that the water carafe on the bedside table was empty. Tomorrow, he thought, the letter will come again, the formal, solicitor's envelope that once a month helped him plan for the future and settle up for the past. Haunted by the horoscope he watched as tobacco smoke curled around his fingers, hearing the street sounds that always irritated him, wondering about his future. This room or another in some other town, a bed in which others had made love, old memories, new patterns of damp. It stretched ahead of him, arranged by magpies, spilled salt or ladders avoided and the position of the planets forty-six years ago.

Near the window his suitcase lay open. He looked at the dirty shirts—he must wash them soon—the small collection of ties. He worried about clothes; appearance was so important. He wondered if he had a blade, hoping that he would not cut himself. At school he had been given a cruel nickname. Molly. He still winced when he remembered.

He stubbed out his cigarette and picked up the book that he had been reading the previous evening. It was set in London but he found no nostalgia in its descriptions of streets and squares. Childhood was featureless, a row of houses that could be anywhere, his mother's complaints about insensitivity and a faint feeling of betrayal.

"She walked up Charing Cross Road", he read, "and stopped a taxi outside Foyles. 'Putney,' she said. The driver turned to look at her. It was almost as if he suspected. His eyes were bloodshot and he needed a shave. 'That's a long way out,' he said. 'I know.'"

Bannister flicked through the pages, reading quickly, looking for the description of love. There was a man in Putney, a couch, a rug but the chapter ended with fingers fumbling awkwardly at buttons.

He got up and went to the window and watched a woman beat a mule. Her face beneath the wide-brimmed mountain hat, was red from the exertion. The panniers on the mule's back were heavily piled with branches and with fruit. Two boys went past, and an old woman dressed in a grey djellaba. The street was narrow and cobbled, an uneven succession of humps and holes and ruts; the roofs of the houses almost entirely covered the brightening blue of the sky. In the archway of the house opposite, a bicycle frame lay rusting, a toy for the children who, as Bannister knew, would soon be swarming around it. It had been there when he came and he suspected that it would still be there when he departed, decaying like the cracked plaster and peeling paint of the houses and the elderly Arabs who lived in them and the fig trees in the courtyards.

He turned away from the window and, with some reluctance, looked in the piece of mirror. A crack in the glass bisected his head in the usual place. He winced. I'm getting old, he thought, forty-six. He had stayed for too long in Tangier, nearly four years avoiding the sun, waiting for his allowance and for love. The face in the mirror stared back at him, dull and immobile, like a figure in a waxworks; the thinning hair, the watering eyes, the loose, soiled collar of his pyjamas. Sometimes he thought that his reflection was like an old photograph of his father. The features were the same but the camera had caught a smugness that Bannister had never felt.

This morning, he thought, I'll go down to the Grand Socco,

have a drink, see if Traynor is back. He was puzzled by the length of the absence, two months in Casablanca on a visit that was supposed to last a week. He could have written, explained what was happening. The face in the mirror twitched slightly. I need a drink, he thought, a gin and tonic. Abu would give him credit. He felt ashamed of this dependence on a people whom he disliked. There would be new tourists in the Grande Socco, off the ferries from Algeciras and Gibraltar. He would watch in the hope and fear of seeing someone whom he knew. A few months before he had recognized a woman but had turned away to avoid her, ashamed of his way of life, his crumpled suit. Respectability had avoided him. It was not easy to keep up appearances.

He looked around the room at the dirty water in the basin, the suitcase, the pile of old newspapers, his coat hanging from a nail behind the door. He would buy a picture when his allowance came. He had been meaning to do so for some time. He could check in the souk for something cheerful; a woodland, perhaps, or a girl.

In the room below an alarm clock rang. She's awake, he thought, earlier than usual. He sat on the bed and listened. The alarm clock was switched off. I think she's fond of me, he thought. He remembered how, yesterday, she had smiled at him on the landing, a towel draped across her shoulders, her hair still wet from the sea. The memory excited him. Her husband is still missing, he thought, gone like Traynor, she probably hasn't heard from him. He imagined her lying in bed, then getting up, putting on a pink dressing-gown, moving around her room. He must speak to her more often, open a kind of friendship. He was almost certain that she would be glad. There was something about the way that she walked, the way that she had smiled at him yesterday that suggested his kind of loneliness. He had heard their fights, the angry, reproachful voice, the tears in the middle of the night. He lay back in the bed aware of the street sounds again. It was going to be a very hot day.

Janet saw, with relief, that the baby was still asleep, his mouth open, his hands tightly clenched. Sunlight searched around his cot. She thought, He's like a lighted exhibit, noticing the veins across his forehead, the swirling particles of dust. She lay and watched him with love and confusion, isolated by his security, knowing that, later in the day, his constant dependence would isolate her even more. Poor little Johnny, she whispered against the pillow, ashamed of her confusion. It was strange that he could sleep through all the noise from the street, the ringing of the clock. Inconsequential sounds, a laugh or a cough would instantly awaken him to bewilderment.

She still felt tired. A swim would be very nice but there was the long walk to the beach, carrying Johnny, being pestered by all those boys. She disliked their mocking faces, their smiles, their insistence, their meaningless, jumbled English. They made her feel like a child left amongst adults, sensing a complexity of emotion that she could not understand. Perhaps it was just money that they wanted. She had never been certain. She was even reluctant to know. Usually they left her when she passed the Rif Hotel but one morning they had followed her across the railway line and stood near to her on the beach, watching in silence, adult in their preoccupation. She had sat there waiting for them to go, fully dressed, annoyed and a little frightened. They had stayed for nearly an hour and then, just as inexplicably, had gone. The incident had cut into her confidence; she remembered it with shame. The boys had not paid her so much attention since then but they would possibly follow her for a while in a mocking suggestion of desire.

She closed her eyes, tightly and seemed to be looking at blood. It isn't fair that he's away, she thought, but the bitterness was less intense. When he came back life might not be any better; love left it still uncharted. A foreign country, she thought, is no place for a baby. The heat and dirt of the town were constant threats to his survival. She opened her eyes and looked across at him, secure in the self-possession of sleep. A cloth book lay on the floor where he had thrown it the previous evening, irritably looking for demonstrations of love. She noticed it with tenderness. He would grow up to know much better towns, away from this ritual of heat. She would save him from sadness; love was a kind of security. One banked away actions and words against the time when one's needs were exposed to open hostility or indifference. Love would give him a future, a sense of survival.

She got quietly out of bed and put on a dressing-gown. He would soon be awake. She kissed his warm forehead and left the room, hoping that she would not meet Bannister on the stairs. There was something sinister about him; his looks, his shuffle, his heavy winter clothes. Sometimes he seemed about to say something but then he would look away again or stare directly at her nervous smile. She went down the stairs to the kitchen. Señora Perez was surrounded by steam. She nodded to Janet.

"You are early," she said.

There was accusation in her voice.

"I'm sorry."

"In Spain it is different." She moved around the kitchen, mourning her lost nationality. "This is a filthy country. Even London, it was not so bad." Her complaints, like the steam, seemed endless. She tightened the strings of her apron.

"I just work and work and work."

On a chair near the door an obese and dusty cat yawned widely and stretched its claws.

"I think Abdul cannot be happy here for very much more." The cat yawned again and stretched and examined Janet with big, malevolent eyes. "They tried to make fire from him last night. They are not Christian," she added, "but that is not a right excuse. No." She banged a kettle on the table. "Six of them. With oil and paper and matches."

"Did they hurt him?"

Janet disliked the cat. It prowled around the house like an enemy observer. She had once found it sleeping on her bed.

"I hurt them," Señora Perez said. Her old face softened

16

with amusement. She was a small woman with hair combed tightly to the back. "They will skip him by the next time, I think." She put the kettle on the floor and wiped her hands against her apron.

"Los hay en todas partes," she said. Her indignation seemed to return like a fever. "Ladnones . . . asesinos . . ."

The cat jumped from the chair and looked suspiciously around the room. It sniffed the steam, its tail erect, then walked across to Señora Perez and rubbed tentatively against her legs.

"He loves me, you see," she said to Janet. "In his tail he has more brains than these people in their heads. Your husband likes him. He told me so himself." She picked up the cat and pressed its head against her shoulder. "Is he still up in the hills?"

She asked the same question every morning.

"He'll be back soon," Janet said. "He went for three weeks. It's almost that now. He's . . ." She hesitated. One could hardly explain. "He's interested in the customs."

"It is not safe up there. They are mad in the heads." The old woman loved disaster. She put down the cat and whispered as if in confidence. "It is not a proper religion. They do not know any better. You see them", she said, pushing the cat away with her foot, "at the bottom of the street down there. Foam at the mouths. Did you ever see that? All those *hombres que rison*? They come down from the hills. Praying to the devil maybe. Who knows?"

On a shelf above the cooker, a chipped statue of the Virgin leaned drunkenly towards a plastic Child of Prague. The morning heat was becoming intense. "All of them heathens!" Señora Perez said, and pushed open a shutter of the window. The street sounds seemed to swell up out of silence, as if a radio had been switched on.

"How is your baby?"

"Fine. He's still asleep."

"He will be waking soon. I have the milk," Señora Perez said. "Fresh. Do not worry. He is good." She looked around for the cat but it had started its morning prowl. "Do not listen to his father, I tell you. Men do not understand. Make sure he grows up a right Catholic. I will give you a holy belt."

She poured some milk into a saucepan.

"Is that Mr. Bannister awake?"

"I think I heard him," Janet said.

"He owes me rent, that man. Complaints, complaints, complaints then he cannot pay. I will be rid of him soon." She put the saucepan on the cooker. "His friend, that Mr. Traynor, has not come back yet. Very strange, I think. Did I tell you", she added, "that he had a pistol in his suitcase? Yes, I saw it there myself."

"He went to Casablanca."

"So he said. Who knows?"

She looked accusingly at Janet. A dog barked outside the window.

"Where is Abdul?" she asked. "Those dogs are savage. They are like the wolves."

She looked out the window and shouted: "Ladnones . . . asesinos!"

The dog continued to bark.

"He is not there. He is too clever for them." She nodded and blessed herself hastily.

"So why would he want a pistol?"

"Maybe for sport," Janet said. She knew Traynor by sight, a tall, embarrassed man who smiled guiltily through the distraction of an erratic twitch in one eye. She had associated him with scholarship not with pistols.

"Sport!" Señora Perez said. She flushed and seemed to grow bigger. "Sport! I know his kind of sport. No good, I tell you. No good at all."

Janet felt tired. One moved through constant confusion. She remembered the boys again. Perhaps they had meant her no harm but their attitude on the beach had seemed so hostile. One could not identify shadows on an unfamiliar landscape.

"I forgot the bottle," she said to break the silence. "I'll go up for it now."

"All right. Very well." Señora Perez had lost interest.

As she climbed the stairs she heard the baby crying. The sound was like a rebuke; it sentenced her to higher standards. Poor little fellow, she thought. There was no escape. The stairs creaked as if in distress and some plaster fell from the ceiling. "Poor little fellow. Don't cry. I'm coming."

Bannister wished that he had been able to find a table in the shade. His gin was warm and had a flat, soft taste. Arabs drank mint tea at the other tables, talking in monotonous whispers. He looked at them with hostility. A car went by, its bumpers red with rust; its brakes shrieked as it swerved to avoid a shoe-shine boy. He finished the drink, wincing at the taste. He wanted to have another but was unsure if his credit would stretch that far. The sun beat down on his dusty shoes, his bald head and his predicament.

The shoe-shine boy was kneeling in front of him before he had a chance to move.

"Yes, boss?"

"No."

"All dusty," the boy said firmly. He put polish on to a rag. "Should be bright. Like Marks and Spencers." He started to polish, muttering with disapproval.

"Oh, all right," Bannister said hopelessly. Each day brought its own small defeats. He sat looking down at the boy's head, wondering if he had enough change.

"English," the boy said. "The Queen. Prince Anne." Looking up he added with what seemed like pride. "Woolworths. Charlie Chaplin."

"Best country," Bannister said solemnly. The boy grinned with incomprehension. "Finest country in the world." Sometimes patriotism flickered like a moment of desire. He tried to recall old history lessons, the red places on the map. "The Battle of Hastings," he said, then paused, for he had forgotten the date. "Best country," he said again, remembering a birthday that he had spent in Blackpool. It had rained heavily all day; the decorations had looked mean and tawdry beneath a low, grey sky. He remembered a solitary walk along the promenade, a trip through the Tunnel of Love.

"Other foot."

The boy polished busily and the Arabs drank their mint tea from small glasses, their muted conversations sounding like the final plotting for revolt. Bannister looked around for Abu. He would have to risk a refusal. Another gin; it was the decisive measure of his indecisive days. If Traynor were back he could have arranged a gentleman's loan. It's all very strange, he thought.

The boy was polishing with a brush. His yellow tee-shirt had a rip on one shoulder and was marked with a faded letter, B. His concentration was disconcerting. Bannister tried to count his change, fingering the coins in his trouser-pocket, hoping that there would not be a scene. His glass had left rings on the table. As he watched, an insect crawled towards them, dragging its squat, red body on probing legs. The coins were warm; when he took his hand from his pocket it was stained blue across the palm. He rubbed it with a dirty handkerchief, looking around with increased dislike at the drinking Arabs, the hot, dusty pavement, the insect crawling towards the rings.

"Over," the boy said, looking up expectantly. "Good job, Charlie."

Bannister took out his change. The small coins were almost worthless. He handed them to the boy.

"Not enough."

"More tomorrow," he said.

One omitted words when talking to a foreigner as if using the language of love. He shifted uncomfortably on the chair, trying to look and feel assured. Sweat seeped from his shoulders and turned cold against his back.

"Now! More now! More now!"

"Tomorrow," Bannister said wearily. He noticed that some men at a nearby table were watching, their dark, unemotional faces betraying no more than a bored interest. A waiter dropped a glass but this diversion did not interrupt their scrutiny. He experienced an old feeling of shame.

"Not enough. All bright."

"Go away," he said, without much hope. A scene seemed unavoidable.

The boy was standing now, the polishing brush held tightly between his hands, his voice becoming more and more incredulous and excited.

"Money, Charlie!"

It was like being back at school, the persecutions in the playground, waiting for the bell to ring and end the daily ordeal. Birthdays should be happier than this. A girl walked past; she might have been amused behind her yashmak. Bannister watched her bitterly, trying to ignore the boy. His tongue seemed swollen and painful. Another gin would make all the difference.

"Money!"

The boy pulled angrily at his knee.

"Go away, I said."

"Money! English bastard!"

He could hit me, Bannister thought, or use a knife, ashamed of his fear and confusion. Violence was the indignity that one most wanted to avoid. Months before, on a street in the medina, he had been forced to see a knife-fight, two men circling each other warily, crouching with hate. He had tried to turn away but a crowd had gathered behind him, pressing him nearer and nearer. Their anticipation had seemed the worst part of violence. "I want to go back," he had said to a woman in a doorway. "I'm not well." But it had been no use. She had pretended not to hear him. Then the crowd had shouted with excitement and against his will he had looked to where one of the fighters was lying crumpled on the street and vomiting into his wound. He remembered the shouts, a boy laughing beside him, a dog barking and the heat trapped between tall, cracked walls.

The boy's fingers tightened on his knee. If he could explain about the allowance, about money, about tomorrow and the envelope from another world. One should not feel so helpless.

"Money! Fuck you, Charlie! Money!"

"Is he annoying you, Mr. Bannister?"

Abu stood beside the table and smiled, revealing startlingly bright gold teeth. "Some accident?" His English was almost perfect.

Bannister said, "I haven't got change." He felt embarrassed at his own relief. "He insisted on polishing my shoes. I didn't want them done in the first place."

Abu smiled again. "Most troublesome," he said. The boy stood silently watching. "It can be very difficult." His air of superiority was always annoying. He was a very tall man; his grey gaberdine cloak hung loosely from sloping shoulders. Bannister disliked him a little more each time they met. Abu pulled out a chair and sat down. "Most troublesome," he said again, folding his arms on the edge of the table. "In England, of course, you polish your own."

"Different customs," Bannister said with resentment.

"Of course. Of course. You are pleased by our customs, are you not, Mr. Bannister?"

"I saw a fight in the medina."

"That's unusual," Abu said, "but these things happen. I dislike them myself, of course. But sometimes . . . unavoidable."

Bannister watched nervously as the boy picked up his box.

"He'll go away now. I must apologize for the trouble. Another drink for you, Mr. Bannister?"

The insect was crawling towards Abu's hand; its legs were awkward and agitated. He killed it with his thumb and casually flicked the small squashed body on to the ground. Bannister said, "A gin." He would never have felt so humiliated with an Englishman. Foreigners expressed their contempt through a ritual of politeness. He had noticed it everywhere he went. It was almost worse, he thought, than angry abuse.

"I'll be settling up tomorrow."

"No, no, this is a gift, shall we say?"

Abu called across to a waiter.

22

"You won't join me for one yourself?"

"Not in public," Abu said and smiled. "In public all eyes are enemies. So they must see mint tea. Five prayers daily and pay the *zekkat*. Religion, Mr. Bannister, is a very effective disguise. Have you found it so?"

"I'm not a believer," Bannister said quickly, then wondered if this were true. "In London I went to seances. My mother was interested."

"The seances?"

"Spirits. Of the dead."

"Most interesting."

"I didn't like them."

He was surprised by the vividness of the sudden childhood memory of a room and a tall woman dressed in black. The room had been the dark back parlour of a suburban house. He remembered the heavy furniture, the unpleasant smell, the other women, his mother beside him at the table holding him tightly by the hand. They had sat in near darkness, for the curtains were drawn, in a silence through which he could hear his own anxious breathing. At the head of the table the woman in black had sat, slumped and motionless. He had wanted to leave. After frightening moans, he remembered, she had started to speak in a low and guttural voice that could have been that of a man. He remembered some of the words. "You haven't forgotten how it used to be? Yes, it's me. Don't you know me? It's me. Just like it used to be?"

"Listen," his mother had said, crying beside him, her hand gripping tighter and tighter. "That's your father speaking."

"Your gin, Mr. Bannister."

Looking up he saw that the boy had gone. The memory was like a dream. Abu smiled.

"I hope you get pleasure from it."

"My allowance comes tomorrow, of course."

"Your friend Mr. Traynor . . ." Abu hesitated. Bannister drank some gin and became conscious again of the heat. It seemed to shimmer before him. "You haven't heard from him?"

"No."

"I'm sure you will quite soon. Mr. Traynor is an interesting man. Don't you think so, Mr. Bannister?"

"I like him," Bannister said uneasily. He feared the result of these intrusions.

"So do I."

The gin had the same unpleasant taste yet one could forget if it had ever tasted better.

"Has Mr. Traynor ever mentioned any association with me?"

Abu's questioning smile reminded Bannister of threats in a playground, small fists clenching.

"An association?"

"Is that, perhaps, the wrong word? An arrangement between us?" The gold glinted brightly again. "A business arrangement?"

"He never mentioned anything."

Abu said, "He's a very good man. He's my friend."

"I didn't know", Bannister said, "of this arrangement." He did not want to know. Acquaintanceship with Traynor was enough. Knowledge could bring too much complexity. Yet he felt curious about the hint in Abu's voice.

"Traynor must have stayed on in Casablanca," he said.

"I think so," Abu said. "A beautiful city but not at this time of the year. Poverty is a problem," he said, pointing. "Don't you agree with me, Mr. Bannister?"

On the pavement Bannister saw an old beggar strapped to some rough boards mounted on wheels. He had no legs. Insects swarmed around his rag-covered stumps. He was pushing himself along with his hands, his face turned blindly towards the sky in a habit of faith or despair. Some boys followed him, laughing. A man threw a coin. It hit against one of the stumps and bounced away, rolling into the gutter. The beggar continued to push himself along. Bannister looked away.

"There is a traditional story," Abu said, "of a blind man who died when he was ordered to do so. He used no violence on himself. He just brought about his death with his own obedience. He had, I suppose you could say, a kind of blind faith. That's a most unusual gift, Mr. Bannister."

The gin was beginning to give him a headache. He could feel the pulse beating in his temples, the start of a dull pressure above his eyes. The glass was almost empty.

"They should stay off the streets."

"May I get you another gin?"

The unoiled wheels creaked slowly along the pavement.

"Tomorrow, of course, I'll . . ."

"No, no, no. Please permit me. I insist."

"Thank you."

Bannister's curiosity emerged like a kind of hope.

"You were saying about Traynor?"

"Yes, of course." Abu ran his fingers across his smoothly shaven chin.

"This association I told you about is to Mr. Traynor's benefit. He makes money from it. You can follow what I say?"

Bannister was glad to feel a little drunk. His confidence expanded.

"You say he makes money," he said, leaning on the table, "for helping you. Am I right so far?" The headache seemed to go away. They're such stupid bastards, he thought, these foreigners, wondering how he could have felt at a disadvantage.

"That is correct."

"For doing what?"

Abu smiled.

"You're jumping ahead of me now, aren't you Mr. Bannister?"

"For what?" Bannister said again, blinking to bring Abu's face back into focus. I shouldn't drink on an empty stomach, he thought.

"You are interested?"

He felt bile stir. "I'd like to know." And the headache started again.

25

"You might like a little extra income? On the same basis as Mr. Traynor."

"For doing what?"

"That same question again. It's not unreasonable, of course. Yet I think, Mr. Bannister, that it might be more wise to leave that aside just now. Until Mr. Traynor returns. Then we can, of course, have a discussion." He stood up. "I hope you enjoyed your drinks."

"Very much."

His confidence was going away.

"Good-day to you, Mr. Bannister."

He pressed his hand against his stomach in an attempt to ease the pain and looked bitterly after Abu. It was going to be a worse day than he had expected.

# Chapter Two

Farrell came up on deck and saw a fishing-boat bobbing near the side of the steamer. The four men aboard it were arguing; their voices came, louder and louder across the water. One was holding a bailing can. As he gestured with it, a wave broke, lashing spray across his back. The others laughed as he bent and bailed out furiously, still shouting. Their voices faded as the *Maroc* moved on with ponderous dignity towards land; some small white dots, a line of pale green mountains, a tentative promise of peace.

"Isn't it hot now?" the American girl said.

He had noticed her earlier across the deck, surrounded by bags and camera equipment, smiling vaguely up at the sun. Her desire for friendship had been like a distress signal; undirected but hopeful. She was dressed for middle age. He had thought of stories about governesses as she sat there, hopeful and ridiculous, displaying her vulnerability to the other passengers. Yet the remark about the heat irritated him. He said "Yes" with unfriendly abruptness, looking away from the small white face, the hair twisted roughly into a bun.

"I saw you in Gibraltar. Near the airstrip. You were having a walk," she said.

"Did you? I don't remember." He did not look at her. He stared down at the steamer's wake, two uneven lines of white foam shaped like a wishbone.

"You wouldn't have seen me," she said. "I was in the Terminal Building."

The Spanish border was just across the airstrip. He remembered the evening then; the line of deserted ground, the shabby little town, the empty bullring and the sad sense of decay. The Rock had been shrouded in mist.

"Did you go to the caves?" she asked. "St. Michael's, isn't it? I was so moved by the music."

He said, without much interest, "I saw them," looking across at her face. It seemed to be curiously innocent. He wondered how years of American life had left it so unshaped. Perhaps she avoided experience, sitting waiting for friendship as emnity and violence passed by.

"I liked them a lot."

She smiled at him as if she were pleased with the answer. He felt that he had passed a test. Some other passengers must have resisted contact by expressions of disagreement. He guessed she was about twenty-five years old.

"I'm going to Tangier," she said. "On vacation." She smiled at him again. He looked towards the land; some beaches, the peaks crouching above Tetuan. Sun rays glanced off the boards of the deck, burning his face and a rail that he was holding. Her hands, he noticed, were small and restless. She said, "I've never been before." The steamer lurched and a piece of luggage went sliding across the deck.

"Neither have I."

A sailor went past with a bucket. His boredom was like a reproach; land seemed to hold no hopes for him. An English tourist took a photograph of his wife who was standing with angular disapproval near a lifeboat.

"Where do you come from?"

The directness of the question appealed to him.

"Ireland."

"Really?"

She seemed to be genuinely interested.

"I know some Irish," she said.

He thought: she's sometimes like Catherine. It was a way of holding her hands, a kind of apprehensive friendliness.

"I'm from San Francisco."

A gull screeched loudly above their heads.

Yet it was easy to imagine what she would be like when she was old, secure in her own inexperience. He guessed that, like other Americans he had known, she would believe pas-

28

sionately in slogans. In God we trust, he thought, looking at her face with its innocently expressed trust in its own attractiveness.

"It's quite an experience, isn't it?" she said.

He wondered what she meant. The boat, perhaps, the sun, the view, or even this unexpected encounter. Making conversation was the penalty one paid for travel; trivia swapped in airports, in bars, and over lunch in strange hotels. Looking for peace one found a new kind of sadness, an inability to make things matter. Only the novelty of places intruded, promising something new until familiarity brought the same feeling of disappointment.

"We're nearly there," he said, looking at his watch.

The white specks had grown into houses. They passed a rusty Spanish trawler, its engine-sound pulsing like an exaggerated heartbeat. The sun rays were fiercer now.

"That must be a minaret," she said, "is it?" pointing towards the town.

He could see old men in cloaks walking aimlessly along the docks. It was foolish to be reminded of someone. It was a form of self-punishment, a nostalgia for failure that released only negative energies. He looked towards the land, the line of green mountains spread protectively behind the town. The European section was white and orderly, the old town a confusing jumble of roofs and walls and towers. The Englishman's camera clicked then clicked again; he would go on recording the obvious. It was always the same. Travel formed small bonds of fraternity and irritation that embarrassed one on arrival.

She said, "I'm staying at the Rif Hotel. I'm told that it's very good."

Her suitcases were piled beside her. The bright labels seemed to boast of sophistication; the identical bedrooms in interchangeable hotels. She did not expect an answer. She took a guide-book from her pocket and said, "There's lots and lots of things to see," flicking trustfully through the pages. He saw the title on the cover. *All You Need to Know about*

29

*Europe and North Africa.* Her lips moved slightly as she read a passage, committing it to memory. He looked away. Irritation was not inevitable. The town came slowly nearer and some of the old excitement awoke. Experience was not the only guide to the future.

He said, "I wouldn't mind a swim," seeing people on the beaches.

"I never learned," she said.

Her innocent smile seemed to challenge him for a moment. He almost volunteered to teach her.

"The beaches sure look inviting. I'm sorry since I came to Europe. But at home we just didn't somehow. Not in our house anyway," she said, with a slight defensiveness.

He wished that he could forget the dream. The smile reminded him but so did an inflection of voice; it robbed some strangers of individuality. Catherine certainly dislikes me, he thought. It was difficult to escape self-pity. It pressed on his excitement, spoiling strange places; it sometimes mocked him like a laugh. But love continued in a recurring dream, images of satisfaction; a closeness that, as he often reminded himself, had never really existed. It was a simplification. She had probably lied as often as he had.

"Where are *you* going to stay?"

"A kind of lodging-house. A friend gave me the address. If they have a room," he said.

"Isn't that rather risky?"

He wondered what she could imagine. Orgies, perhaps, or drugs. Her innocence would not be without a certain regret.

"I don't imagine so."

"I read about Tangier in novels. You know. But it probably isn't like that at all."

"Like what?"

"Oh, you know. Drugs and that. And rape in every alley."

He laughed. "We'll soon see, won't we?"

She looked at her guide-book again.

"In the Café de Paris," she told him, "in the gracious Place de France, you can mingle with countless celebrities."

The bar smelled strongly or urine. The waiter's arm was tattooed with an obscenity. He said, "The hell I do," to a small old man who was leaning against the counter. "You want to know somethin'? The hell I do. Now or never. And that's bloody that." The old man murmured something in agreement. The waiter's voice was harsh and belligerent; he might have been heckling a crowd. The bottles on the shelf behind him glinted faintly in the light from an electric bulb. The door and shutters were closed. On the floor, near Farrell, a listless dog scratched itself, its mournful head at an angle, its tongue protruding. The waiter's voice went on, cutting through the heat, rising towards boastfulness.

"I could tell you about Traynor so I could. I know a bloody sight more than the bastards think."

The dog dragged itself slowly towards Farrell's suitcase and examined it, sniffing loudly. In a room above their heads a man began to shout. The waiter paused for a moment.

"That's Durcan," he said.

The senseless shouting was like a part of the heat; they seemed to merge together. Farrell finished his beer and went out into the daylight. The suitcase was heavy in the heat. He climbed some steps, past the stall of a metalsmith, hearing Moorish music on a radio. In a stall near the top of the steps an elderly man was mending or making sandals. He looked at Farrell but his glance was entirely meaningless; it might have been hostile or friendly. Near his feet some leather shavings lay like rusted springs. On the outskirts of the market boys ran, recklessly, between baskets of melons and muscatel grapes. A water-seller rang a bell and people came in steady procession from an archway in the medina wall. The smell of mimosa was like nostalgia, evocative of other places seen for the first time, other times of hope. A pilgrim limped past, his hooded head lowered, his dusty robe trailing behind him like a public penance. Farrell put down his suitcase and thought of the American girl. He had left her safe, in a taxi going trustfully towards her hotel. Her name was Susan. "After my grandmother," she had told him. He knew that this irrelevancy

31

would remain in his mind long after he had forgotten her face. Sunlight glinted on the minarets and annoyed the harassed donkeys held by overdressed Riff women. Some children were following a tourist, making his progress almost impossible, guiding him back towards the wall of the medina. He tried to ignore them but his broad red face was worried. "Charlie Chaplin!" they shouted and then, as if in some doubt, "Tom Mix!" Farrell tried to imagine the stuffy cinemas, the forgotten films jumping erratically before an eager audience. The innocent cruelty of children was universal.

The tourist said, "Hello. You're English aren't you? What a day!" He stared through spectacles at the jostling children and an old man holding a snake. The sleeves of his shirt were rolled up past his elbows. He had a handkerchief knotted on his head.

"They won't let you do what you want to," he said bewildered. "And I seem to have lost my wife. She was with me a few minutes ago." He peered myopically around the crowded market. "Quite a large woman. In a blue dress," he said. "She's of a nervous disposition."

"I'm sure she'll find you if you stay here."

"I certainly hope so. The coach leaves shortly, you see." He scratched the handkerchief. "It's so annoying," he said sadly. A small boy reached to touch his camera. "This is the kind of thing. No, I'll go back to where I last saw her. I'm much obliged to you for your help."

He moved away, the children swarming around him. Gulls twisted in the glittering sky.

One could stay too long here, Farrell thought, but the feeling of isolation was like a tonic. Tomorrow brought no routine, no familiar irritations. It was almost as if one had not got a past. He watched the knotted handkerchief bobbing aimlessly amongst the crowd, like some old sign of respectability that has lost all meaning. There was something about the fidelity of the quest that reminded him of another world, a world so easily forgotten in the heat and this orderless bustle. Appointments kept and broken, the alarm-clock going off were, like the woman in the blue dress, somewhere else. It was a new kind of selfishness that mattered. There were few mistakes that one could make, less responsibility for actions. It was like a fundamental religion; one could make one's own rewards. One wasn't on trial before one's own regrets or Catherine crying in a bar.

He picked up his suitcase and went to look for the house in which he hoped to stay. The route had been drawn for him on an envelope. Away from the market place, the pitch of living quietened; men conversed calmly in pavement cafés. Through some open doors he could see cool courtyards, a fountain, a woman preparing food. As the streets grew more narrow the heat returned and thick, white dust made it difficult to breathe with comfort. The handle of his suitcase burned against his palm. He turned a corner into a short, cobbled street and knocked on the door of a house. A cat brushed smoothly against his legs.

"Yes?"

"Señora Perez?"

The old woman seemed reluctant to agree. She looked across his shoulder as if expecting to see someone else. Behind her he could see a large, dim hallway, narrow, uncarpeted stairs. Her old hands fumbled restlessly with a loose string on her apron.

"My cat," she said. "Where did you find him?"

"He must have been at the door here."

The cat pushed past her feet and merged with the dimness.

"If you are looking for that Mr. Traynor he is not here," she said, half-closing the door. "Maybe he won't be here ever again." She smiled with a kind of satisfaction.

"No, I'm hoping to rent a room."

"From me?"

Her suspicion came out of the dimness like a noise in the night. She looked down carefully at his suitcase. He wondered why the name Traynor seemed familiar then remembered that the waiter in the bar had used it.

"I do not know," Señora Perez said. Her lips moved silently as if in prayer.

Farrell said, "A friend of mine. Cummins. You may remember him. He stayed here for a while last year. He told me you might have a room."

"I remember a Mr. Cummins. He came from Ireland."

"That's right. I'm from Ireland as well."

It was like producing a passport to have it stamped with signs of approval. One's nationality took on a new importance when one was away from home. It stayed with one like an accent, crossing all frontiers, gaining a spurious relevance.

"I know about Ireland," she said suspiciously.

She opened the door more widely; sunlight trailed across the dusty black and white tiling of the hall.

"There is a room. That Mr. Traynor. Who knows if he will ever be back again. In the wardrobe he has a few things but they can be stored." Her lips moved silently. She said, "If you like you can see it," and turned before he could answer. He followed her slowly up the stairs. The house smelled heavily of dust; there was a feeling of heat trapped uselessly in the old dark corners of rooms. On the first landing she paused beside a plastic font and shook holy water indiscriminately down the front of her apron.

"In this room here there is an Irish girl," she said, "married to an Englishman." Farrell sensed some disapproval.

"Her husband is up in the hills. Strange but not my concern. Nobody listens to me now. They think they know about everything."

She went on up the creaking stairs.

"Mr. Bannister is here in this one. You are the next one."

Her disapproval seemed to be growing.

"Nobody listens," she said again. She took a key from the ledge above a door. "I keep it locked for him when he is away. He said a week. That is months ago now. Who will pay me the rent?" She unlocked the door. "It is a nice little room. Yes? Very peaceful." She opened the shutters of a small window and said, "The street" as if announcing a discovery.

34

The room was small; an iron bedstead in one corner, a wash-stand, a single uncomfortable chair. The wardrobe was near the window.

"His things are there," she said.

Farrell noticed a pair of shoes beneath the bed. It reminded him of Paddington hotels, rooms rented by day or night; a gas meter, a list of rules, a mirror near the bed were all that were missing. Traynor lived simply. The only personal touch was a copy of the *Daily Mirror* left folded on the wash-stand.

"I could get you new sheets and some blankets."

She stood looking down at the bed as if mourning a corpse. "Mr. Traynor had a rug. Are you sure", she asked, "you are Irish?" She seemed accustomed to deceit. He wondered what Traynor had done to annoy her. The room did not hold any clues, the shoes had a peculiar innocence. One could easily imagine his loneliness but not his duplicity.

He said, "Yes, I'm from Dublin," looking down to the street where a boy swayed on a bicycle. "My name is Farrell. This would suit me very well indeed. Could I have it for three or four weeks?"

"If he comes back," she said, "he has no rights here. It is my room. I own it."

She looked around with what might have been pride. On the wall near the window the plaster was flaking with dampness. "There was a picture of the Holy Infant there. He took it down. I will put it back."

"Please don't go to any trouble."

"Not any trouble. Brings good luck to a house," she said.

He could imagine her lighting candles, making a bargain. He knew the comfort it brought. One could envy a version of faith without believing in it. Cummins had told him about her.

"Was Mr. Traynor here on holidays?"

He was surprised at his own curiosity. She went to the door. She could have been checking to see if there was anyone on the landing like a peasant woman being cautious before describing her landlord.

35

"That is what he said. I do not believe it." Her eyes, he noticed, were unusually dark. Standing near the door, she said, "But of course it is not my concern."

There was something oddly comic in her protestations. "All the same," she said, then stopped and nodded her head, pursing her lips as if determined to say no more.

He said, "There's an Irish girl downstairs?"

"There is Mrs. Merton. You will hear her baby maybe. But it does not cry so loudly. It is a good child. It is two stairs down so that is all right," she said. She went out to the landing. "I will get the sheets then I tell you about the rent." He heard her creaking down the stairs, past the other doors and the cheap holy water font, a journey of faith and suspicion.

He went to the window again. Two children sat solemnly on the opposite pavement examining a small white object. It looked like an egg. He could hear their precise voices; they were imitating their parents. In the archway of the house behind them, a bicycle frame, rusted and obscure, looked like something one saw on a beach when the tide went out. He could hear faint sounds from the market and, off in the distance, the wail of a siren. Some streaks of cloud were gathering in the section of the sky that he could see above the roof-tops. A spider scurried along the window-ledge and clambered out of view, two legs like grappling-irons, disappearing last. A man came up the street. He was wearing a heavy overcoat. Sunlight glinted on his highly polished shoes. The children stopped talking and watched him with interest, nudging each other in complicity. The man coughed loudly; they immediately imitated him with choking, gasping coughs. He came into the house. Farrell heard Señora Perez's voice raised shrilly in the hallway then the stairs creaked loudly and the door of the room beneath his own was banged. He thought, that's Bannister, and moved away from the window. He always disliked unpacking. The case was full of crumpled clothes, a few paperbacks, some European cigarettes. He had packed hastily.

On the previous night, in Gibraltar, he had stayed late in

36

the Rock Hotel drinking with the other journalists who had been there covering the Referendum. The town had been gay with Union Jacks, hanging from window to window, with pictures of the Queen and the Duke of Edinburgh and banners reading 'Keep the Rock British'. Even the taxis had been decorated with posters and with flags. As the drivers brought their fares to the frontier-post to look across at Spain, the shabbiness of the bullring must have helped their patriotism. He had filed some cynical reports. The Union Jacks were over duty-free shops that had windows crammed with cameras; he had described the tourists coming ashore to buy cigarettes and watches and pints of British beer. In a cable-car, going to the summit of the Rock, he had overheard two English women talking about the Queen, proud that her portrait was so widely displayed, unaware that it was commerce that counted. The Catholic bishop had prayed in procession that a wise decision might be made but he, like everyone else, must have felt fairly certain that God would continue to approve good business arrangements. Up on the Rock, past the Barbary apes and the old naval observation posts, Farrell had looked across at Africa, some mountain peaks in a mist, and waited for the count to finish. The boats in the harbour had been like toys, a yacht was a white triangle against the streaked and silent sea. He had looked down at gulls swooping deftly around ledges, their cries coming up like implorings. They might have been the damned were it not for the sun, and the haze and the wide, steady tilt of their wings. He had looked across at Africa with interest and with hope. One could fasten such belief in the unknown.

He took some clothes from his suitcase and left them on the bed. The front door banged and he heard a girl's voice, "Very nice, thanks, Señora Perez. They looked after Johnny in the café. I don't suppose that anyone was looking for me?"

"Nobody, nobody," Señora Perez said. "He will be back soon. He will get over his foolishness."

"I'm going to lie down for a while."

Farrell opened the door of the wardrobe. A smell of moth-

37

balls spread slowly across the room. A few old sports jackets were draped across hangers, their shoulders sloping with the line of past defeats. Traynor favoured tweeds; the round, leather-patched elbows recalled country clubs and golf courses and the persistent smell of chalk. One could almost picture the man, an affability, a tie from a minor public school. He closed the door and went back to the window. Señora Perez was coming up the stairs.

"I wish I'd brought my book," Susan said, looking unhappily at the menu. "They warn you about some foods. All that spice and things." She looked around the restaurant as if hoping that there might be a copy on some shelf. Her stock of trust seemed unable to cope with the absence of hamburgers. She said, "It's so easy to make a mistake."

Three Arabs in elaborate costumes played monotonous music on two flutes and a flat and echoing drum. The drummer was small and bored. He peered, without interest, into the beam of a moving spotlight, his fingers tapping out a rhythm that occasionally matched that of the flutes. It was like a form of protest but the others did not seem to care. The wailing notes went on above the heads of the people sitting at tables, the red-robed waiters, the small boys pushing big trolleys, the stout woman at the cash desk.

"I think I know what some of it means," Farrell said. "*Tajin* is a kind of pigeon stew."

"Pigeon! You couldn't mean ordinary pigeons?"

"Or you might prefer the mutton. It's supposed to be excellent here."

She said, "I certainly would."

The drummer increased the pace of his tappings. The pictures of palm trees and camels on the wall were almost hidden by shadows. Two tourists were attempting to dance. Cigarette smoke swirled frantically in the beam of a spotlight. One of the dancers stumbled and her partner laughed with loud, hollow amusement. Farrell drank some wine and said, "Your hotel seems nice."

38

"Oh yes. I like it."

She smoked awkwardly, her eyes watering as she tapped ash nervously to the floor. A large charm bracelet jangled on her wrist; small hearts and elephants, a train, a horse, a telephone, a book marked Holy Bible. She smiled across the smoke, the flickering flame of the squat red candle and said, "I got such a surprise when I saw you."

She had been writing postcards in the lounge, an address book open before her, stamps scattered on a chair.

"I supposed we'd probably meet but not so soon."

"I've been looking forward to it," he said.

She accepted the lie trustfully. On the way back from the beach he had passed her hotel and decided that being with her would be better than being alone.

She said, "I like the wine," but did not sound convinced. Her glass was almost full.

"There's a phrase-book at the back of my guide," she said. "I wish I hadn't left it back at the hotel."

He wondered what phrases she wanted. "You'll find", he said, "that I have quite good English."

She stared at him a moment before laughing.

"Yes, but has anyone else? I nearly went mad over there in Spain."

She looked some years younger. Her dress was not so deliberately severe. The charm bracelet jangled as she stubbed out her cigarette. A waiter took their order, giving little bows of mute approval as he sucked the top of his pencil and laboriously wrote down each course. His beard was stained with flecks of nicotine, his red robe frayed at the cuffs and elbows. He reminded Farrell of a rather disreputable Santa Claus in a supermarket. He gave a final bow before leaving, backing away from them, smiling at the floor. The flute music wailed up and then subsided like a keen. The wine was sharp and bitter. Farrell asked, "How long will you stay here?" and noticed Catherine's trick, the nervous movement of hands, the way that she looked away.

"Couple of weeks. Then I'll go to Casablanca."

She fidgeted with the stem of her glass, revolving it between her fingers and thumb. "That music", she said, "is getting on my nerves. But I like it here, don't you?" she added politely.

"There's a floor-show later," he said.

The waiter brought fish soup. She said, "It *is* good" with such a childish pleasure that he felt a sudden tenderness.

"Do you always travel by yourself?"

"Oh not always. This year though. I think I prefer it."

"It's a long way to Casablanca, you know."

"Not as far as it is to San Francisco."

"True."

At a nearby table a drunk began to get angry; his voice rose dogmatically. "Not if I say you can't." A friend tried to reason with him; the anxious voice went on repeating something over and over again but the drunk said, "Not if I say you can't. I'm not an unreasonable man, am I? I've never been accused of that."

Farrell wondered, as tenderness turned to desire, if it was merely the old convention; the flickering candle and music and heat. He had learned to distrust impulsive feelings; old guilts reawakened with them, like bad memories. There could be no real attraction.

She said, "How long are you staying?"

It was almost as if she had guessed but when he told her she nodded with polite interest. Desire gave one a past. One travelled back through the almost forgotten feelings. He drank more wine and listened to the low steady tap of the drum. One looked back with sentiment to times and feelings of pain and of distortion. It was still possible to feel a pang of jealousy.

The waiter served mutton from a wooden dish. Susan said, "I might get to see Ireland." He told her a little about Dublin. Her guide-book would contain all the places that must be seen. It was easy to turn a city into a museum.

The floor-show started, the flutes wailing as a man in native costume danced amongst the tables, a brass tray balanced on his head. Candles and wine glasses on the tray tilted and straightened as the dancer moved his body. He passed their table. Drops of sweat were leaving deep tracks down the grease-paint on his forehead. He was not wearing shoes. "That's very skilful," Susan said, watching with admiration. Farrell searched his pockets for matches. The dancer finished. The drunk applauded loudly. She refused a cigarette. He looked at his watch. It was almost eleven. "You must be tired," he said.

"Not really."

A small elephant jangled against the Bible.

She said, "I slept late this morning."

The lights went out. When a single spot came on a girl was standing between the tables. She raised her arms above her head and the music started again, in a faster rhythm, pulsing through the darkness like the sound of an oncoming train. The girl swayed from side to side; her hair almost covered her face. The drum beat quickened. A long thin scar on her shoulder glowed blue against the smooth brown of her skin. Her head fell back until her hair was almost trailing against the floor. She moved her stomach and breasts, her legs wide apart, her head jerking as if in anguish. The people applauded in time to the drum beats. "This Moorish girl", a voice said over the microphone, "is celebrated throughout the land. She has danced before the King." The message was repeated in French. The girl stood straight, hands high above her head but continued to sway her breasts, her mouth half-open in what might have been the beginning of a smile.

"I'd like a cigarette," Susan said. Her disapproval was almost comic. It was as if she had, for the first time, encountered a hint of unAmerican activities. Holding a match for her Farrell wondered about the roots of her innocence.

She inhaled and said, "It's a bit obvious, isn't it?"

"I suppose so."

The girl clapped her hands very gently and smiled, jerking her body roughly in a crude parody of love. It meant as much and as little as an uninvolved encounter; the body responding to the act, the mind remaining disinterested. Her teeth were pressing on her lower lip. The pretence of pleasure was like a familiar disguise for that painful sort of failure, the mind that did not care. She shuddered and the lights went out. Susan said, "I am a little tired."

Farrell got the bill. The waiter said, "We welcome you again." The drunk was singing badly as they went out to the street. His mournful voice followed them. She said, "Thank goodness for fresh air" looking up at the green-tinged sky. A slight breeze rustled the leaves of the palm trees in the gardens of the Place de France. They walked down the Boulevard Pasteur towards the sea front, past the banks and the European shops. A neon light hissed and flickered above the door of a tourist office. He said, "I hope you don't mind the walk." The constraint between them was like the start of bitterness. She said, "No, I like it." It was almost as if they had fought.

"We go down this way, I think."

She walked along slowly, her hands in the pockets of her coat; he knew that she was thinking about the dance. The body in the light, the jerking, pointless act had fashioned some faint resentment. If we slept together, he thought, it would be like this, the same feeling of disappointment. A moth brushed past his face. On the seafront, the music from the strip-clubs was brash with false excitement. A line of bright orange lights in the harbour betrayed the position of a ship. Outside her hotel he said, "I'm sure I'll see you again." She smiled with what might have been relief.

"Oh, yes. I'd like that. Thanks a lot."

Her innocence was returning. Now that fear was gone she could offer new vulnerability.

"I enjoyed it very much."

He watched her crossing the foyer. The breeze from the sea was surprisingly cold. He thought about Catherine and the dancer's body as he walked back towards his room and felt desire again, uncontrolled and useless, like an old feeling of loss. Señora Perez had left the front door open. The smell of damp in the hall, the creaking staircase had an odd familiarity. It almost seemed like home.

He opened the door of his bedroom. The man's fist hit him

on the left side of his head. The force of the blow knocked him back on the landing. He tried to avoid a kick, seeing the dark frightened face and the boot coming towards him. It caught him on the shoulder. He thought, I've got to get up and felt a trickle of blood from his eye. The man hesitated. The pain in his shoulder spread quickly along his arm. He closed his eyes and heard the man run down the stairs.

I must be a coward, he thought. I should have stopped him. I should. . . . He heard Bannister cough and call, "Is anything wrong up there?" The front door banged.

He opened his eyes and stood up, leaning against the wall for support. The pain spread sharply across his chest. The blood was warm against his cheek and chin. The sound of his breathing startled him; a rasping sound that went on like someone else's grief. He switched on the light. The wardrobe door was open, the sports coats scattered on the floor. Their linings had been ripped open; the pieces of thread and canvas were like withered entrails. He went into the room and sat on the bed.

# Chapter Three

"My letter," Bannister said, looking forlornly around the kitchen. "It always arrives at this time. Are you quite certain?"

Señora Perez banged down a saucepan. "Ah letter, letter. Why now for letter, letter?"

Bannister loosened the knot on his tie and peered through the steam. These foreigners were impossibly difficult. Small wars were waged everywhere one went; attacks were launched without provocation.

"I just thought that it might have arrived. I'll settle up the rent, or course." He hoped that this would placate her. "Perhaps you'd let me have your account."

"Your letters and accounts!"

He had dreamed of violence, confused and disturbing as always; a man vomiting in the medina, the shoe-shine boy appearing beside his mother at a seance. His mother had smiled and said, "That's your father." The boy had laughed threateningly. "Come on now, Charlie." He awoke, trapped by heat, in the narrow bed, to the sound of footsteps on the stairs.

"Do you think I have no worry on my head but letters and accounts? After last night happening, you think?"

"I heard some noises," Bannister said.

"Noises in this house? You did. Everyone heard them noises. Everyone but me who owns it." She used her apron to wipe sweat from her forehead.

"When were there noises in this house before?"

Bannister looked at some statues on a shelf and was reminded of Christmas windows; the cheap, crude plaster figures gathered around the child who was supposed to save the world. He remembered a Christmas Eve in London, a

44

cold, grey drizzle in Oxford Street, a group of women singing carols sadly as they rattled their collection boxes. He said, "Those statues . . ." wondering vaguely if they meant anything but she was not listening.

"It never happened before," she said. "This is a holy house. The priest has blessed this very kitchen." A kettle boiled over, the water hissing and steaming on the red-hot electric plate.

"I believe I heard someone running."

"He tried to murder Mr. Farrell," she said.

"I don't think", Bannister said, "that I've met Mr. Farrell."

"He is staying in the room where that Mr. Traynor was. Only since yesterday." She blessed herself hastily. "We might all have been murdered."

She opened a window. The steam poured out like smoke into the noisy street.

"And what did the police say?"

"The police? They did not say anything. They have not been told. I would not trust them. Have you seen them? Every kind of robber. To call them police is to make me laugh." She looked away, shaking her head. "Esas cosas ya las se yo," she said. "Fui a la escuela!"

"I think," Bannister said nervously, "that we ought to be doing something about it." He noticed with surprise that he had included himself as a participant in a plan. He was not asked often for an opinion yet the desire to be included had not worn away at café tables or in shabby rented rooms. One went on hoping.

"Perhaps", he suggested, "the Spanish Consul . . ."

"It is my business only."

"But if someone was trying to kill someone."

Bannister seldom considered death. It was an abstraction; prayers, a tasteful wreath, some verses in a newspaper. Life provided enough disappointment for thought.

Señora Perez closed the window. She wiped her hands on her apron and said, "I know what to do."

45

Hopes of complicity and pleasant involvement faded like the steam.

"Is this fellow Farrell an Englishman?"

"He is from Ireland."

Señora Perez took down a statue and balanced it carefully on the palm of her hand. Bannister watched with embarrassment, as she said with affection, "The golden child. He helps me. He is my friend."

It was like hearing voices at a seance; one feared, above all, that it might be true.

"Ever since that Mr. Traynor," she said. "Things have been no good."

Bannister remembered his talk with Abu.

"Funny that Traynor is still away."

"Not funny at all."

"Well I don't exactly mean funny. Odd is the word."

She kissed the statue and put it back on the shelf. I never liked that fellow Abu, he thought. He's crooked like all the rest of them. Traynor was mad to get involved with him. If he is involved. He coughed and Señora Perez's cat rubbed roughly against his leg.

"About my letter."

"It is over there", she said, "on the table."

"So it did come. I thought it would."

Seeing the British stamp was like meeting an old and valued friend. There were new possibilities each time.

"I'll get this cashed now," he said, working out, as he did each month, the value in dirhams. He wanted a gin and tonic. Abu could go to hell. Traynor was a fool. Or worse.

"Good-day, to you, Señora," he said.

The old woman ignored him.

Farrell finished shaving and went back to the window. The sunlight hurt his eyes. His shoulder was stiff and painful. He saw a cat stalk arrogantly across the street and pause in an open doorway as if afraid to enter. The heat was getting worse; a faint smell of decay came up from the street.

46

Standing at the window he tried to remember the face of the man who had attacked him. It was no use. The only features he could remember would fit a thousand faces; eyes dilated with fear, a narrow line of moustache, and big and uneven teeth. The incident was losing reality. Perhaps one forgot about fear in the way one tried to forget about love.

He went downstairs. Señora Perez said: "You are happy about our talk, Mr. Farrell?"

"Oh yes. That's fine," he said, looking at the girl who was with her.

"It is the best thing to forget. The police here are bad. You do not know them. I would not want them in my house. Spying around. And more." She lowere her voice. "It would be different if they could be trusted but they can not."

"I was sorry to hear what had happened," the girl said. "Señora Perez told me. I hope you weren't hurt."

"It wasn't much."

"Such louts and ruffians," Señora Perez said. "In Spain it would not be possible. When I was living in London there were louts there as well but never so bad. Never."

"I didn't hear anything," the girl said. "I went to bed early."

"Señora Perez tells me you're from Ireland."

"Yes. From Dublin."

"You do not know Mrs. Merton. This is Mr. Farrell." The old woman shook her head angrily. "After last night I forget. Who will blame me? Louts, all of them."

She went into the kitchen. "You'll keep an eye on Johnny?" the girl said.

"Of course, of course. Many times I have said it already."

"It might be too warm for him, even in the café."

"Forty years ago I knew about babies. This one is no different. He will be all right."

"You're going to the beach?" Farrell asked. She nodded. She was carrying a neatly rolled towel.

"Señora Perez is looking after my baby."

"May I walk down with you?"

47

"Of course. Isn't it odd", she said in the street, "how we should meet out here? And both of us come from Dublin."

"This man Traynor . . ." he said, curiously.

"I don't really know him. Do you? He looks like a teacher."

They paused at a corner to allow a van go by, its engine labouring heavily. She was wearing a blouse and old, blue corduroy jeans.

"It's funny about last night, isn't it? Do you think it had something to do with Mr. Traynor?"

"I wouldn't know."

She laughed.

"What a way to start a holiday!" she said.

The light burned painfully against his eyes. He closed them, walking blindly for a moment but when he opened them again the glare was worse. The streets were almost deserted. The sound of children playing came from narrow archways. A few unkempt dogs moved listlessly on the pavements, their tails dragging heavily in the thick, white dust. The heat was like a threat; it surrounded one with a feeling of insufficiency.

"He was friendly with Mr. Bannister," she said. "They used to go drinking together."

A dog exposed its teeth and snarled, rolling its invalid eyes. They crossed the street to avoid it.

"I'm so nervous", she said, "about Johnny. There's so many things that could happen to him here. He isn't five months old yet."

"It must be difficult."

"You have no idea," she said.

He wanted to know about her husband but avoided asking the question.

"It isn't easy. There are all kinds of extra things to worry about. Diseases I'd never heard of."

They were walking through busier streets. Beggars had gathered at the corners. A woman in front of them carried a goose under each arm.

"It's strange town," Farrell said.

It was not like talking to Susan. There was no easy detachment; he felt a sense of advantages lost or gained. The geese hissed foolishly, craning their necks from imprisonment. He tried to imagine her husband, looking for signs as if a picture could be formed from her step or the way that she held her head Relationships left their traces, tentative reactions, a defensive laugh or smile; the armoury of self-protection.

"I'd swop it for Dublin," she said with no obvious bitterness.

"Have you been here long?"

"A couple of months."

He could find no hints yet he knew that too often one gave nuances the meanings that one wanted them to have. One had to be careful. They walked past hotels on the sea front. The empty night-clubs stood like monuments to ancient satisfactions, their unlighted neon signs like old, worn letters on a tomb. An old man offered them hashish. "Of the very best stuff!" he said imploringly. Beneath a fez his face was deeply lined.

"Not now."

"I've smoked some of it," Janet said. "It's so cheap here. But not since David went away."

He knew a name now. In some obscure way this knowledge caused a feeling of resentment. It was like an intrusion.

"I can't get over last night," she said. He opened a gate and they went across a railway line to the beach. "It must have been terrible, a fright like that. Not to talk of the bruise and that." The horn of a diesel engine was sounded in the distance.

"I didn't get time to be frightened."

"All the same. It's no joke. I don't know what I'd have done."

The tide was in; a light breeze flapped against the umbrellas over iron tables. Bathers had staked out claims on the sand; towels and clothes were spread like tokens of possession. A beach-ball knocked against their feet. Farrell kicked it towards a group of children. The face painted on it bounced grotesquely away, grinning up at the cloudless sky.

D                                    49

"I usually go farther up the beach," she said. "It's more private."

"Wherever you like to go."

Sand worked its way into their shoes. The train passed, a guard leaning dangerously from a window watching the line ahead. The small carriages clanged noisily together.

"It goes to Casablanca," she said.

"Where Traynor is?"

"You'll have to ask Mr. Bannister about him."

"What's he like?"

"Bannister?" She grimaced. "Odd. He makes me feel uncomfortable. Anywhere here is grand."

They sat down awkwardly.

"I hope", she said, "that Johnny is all right. I sometimes leave him in that café." She pointed towards a small, white building, with an ice-cream sign hanging crookedly above the door. "The woman in there looks after him while I'm swimming." Her loyalty to the baby was like a strange custom. He found it difficult to grasp its implications.

"Señora Perez", he said, "seemed confident."

"Oh she's good that way. She's kind-hearted really. Did she ask you if you go to mass?"

"No. Not yet. Will she?"

"She will."

"I must prepare a convincing answer."

The sand was hot and uncomfortable.

"My husband's not religious", she said, "in the conventional sense." She ran sand through her fingers. "But he has an interest in Islam." She looked towards a man and boy who had sat down near by. "Señora Perez doesn't approve."

"I gathered that she didn't exactly espouse the Arab cause," Farrell said.

The man undressed slowly, folding each piece of clothing carefully on a towel. The boy looked away from him, staring for a moment at Janet with dark, disillusioned eyes. He was Arab. The man's white stomach hung heavily above his togs. He put on large sun-glasses.

50

Janet said, "You aren't going to swim this morning?"

"I forgot to bring anything," Farrell said. "But it doesn't matter. I can come down later in the day."

"I always prefer it at this time. It's usually more private. There are boys . . ." she said.

The man's arm was resting across the boy's shoulders. He was talking eagerly. They could hear some words. ". . . and afterwards a café somewhere. A place you'd like . . ." The precise English accent with its cadences of enthusiasm seemed strangely foreign in the heat. "Or perhaps in the morning . . ." The boy shrugged casually and stared out across the sea, the arm moving on his shoulders like a swaying burden. ". . . I could hire a car . . ."

"But you'll swim, I hope," Farrell said. "I don't want to spoil it for you."

She smiled. "I'd love to. Not that I'm very good."

He sensed her embarrassment and closed his eyes.

Like a belief in God the town and beach became more defined in the darkness. It was not just the opposite of what one knew, the outlines of familiar life: it was more like a series of hints. One saw, through an unfamiliar prism, emotions one recognized distorted into new clarity. Self-knowledge seemed to be infinitely possible in the simplified surroundings of a place that held no memories. The hints were in new streets, and sounds and one's instinctive reactions.

"I could almost sleep," he said. He did not open his eyes; he could hear her undressing beside him.

"Why don't you?"

"On the other hand . . ." the man's voice sounded less certain, a little more urgent, ". . . a trip to the mountains. We could have a packed lunch." It was a voice that could sink to despair. "I believe they're worth seeing."

"Well I'll be seeing you."

He watched her walk down to the sea. The sunlight seemed brighter. Her footsteps left prints near the edge of the water. He wanted to call after her, a tender apology for the meaningless triteness of their talk but the words and the tone were elusive and she probably did not care. She stood letting spent waves break thinly around her ankles. A child laughed as someone's sandcastle collapsed. A boat pushed away from a ship in the harbour and moved towards the jumbled docks, its engine droning peacefully. She walked in deeper, cautiously testing the water. Her skin was lightly tanned; the yellow bathing suit seemed garish against her legs and shoulders, the fairness of her hair. He closed his eyes again and the man's voice went on towards desperation. Love moved furtively in the lonely places. He remembered being attacked. When he looked again she was swimming awkwardly, keeping close to the beach. She looked like a child, defiantly splashing in the waves. He wished that he had called to her. The thought of her husband stirred like an insult in his mind; the sun burned on like jealousy and the children shrieked, playing carelessly across the hot, white sand. "If that's what you'd like then of course we can do it." The man leaned and kissed the boy awkwardly on the cheek. The boy moved away from him, looking at Farrell with a cynicism that he should not have possessed. The man coughed and said something, speaking quietly now that he was aware of being watched. He scratched the back of his neck and stared, embarrassed, at the tops of his fat, white knees.

Janet came out of the water. She waved to him, shaking water from her arms.

"Did you like it?" he asked as she came nearer, noticing that the boy was watching her with interest.

"It was lovely."

She knelt beside him. Small drops of sea-water came from her costume and ran down the inside of her thighs. Her wet hair was dark. She said:

"It's so cool. You're really missing it."

The man collected his clothes and walked quickly away.

"I'm going to take a swim later."

The boy hesitated then followed, uncertainly. She put a towel around her shoulders and said, "It almost makes the heat worth while."

"You swim well," he said.

There was something protective, like pity, in the need he felt to praise her.

"Oh, I'm not very good at all. Ordinary."

"You're better than I am," he said truthfully. She laughed and started to dry her shoulders, pulling the towel against them. "I'm sure that isn't true."

Her breasts moved beneath the tight, wet costume. The man was out of sight.

"What part of Dublin do you come from?" he asked.

"Glasnevin. Do you know it?"

"Vaguely."

"We had a flat there. Lindsay Road. We gave it up when we came to Morocco." She covered herslf with the sand-flecked towel. "If you wouldn't mind looking away."

The boy was walking slowly along the beach, his hands in the pockets of his jeans. He looked like a sea-bird searching for something, a dark shape on the sand. The boat went back towards the ship in the harbour; another group of tourists would be waiting to disembark.

"I'll soon be a day here," Farrell said. The pain in his shoulder was easing. He looked at his watch. "It seems much longer than that."

"I'm sure it does," she said, "after last night and everything."

A train was shunting in the distance. The sound came, muted, like gun-fire in the hills. The boy's dejected shape had gone from the beach. A pedlar walked along the shoreline. He was carrying leather bags and a tray of ornaments that glittered cheaply in the sun. He extolled them in a high and hopeless voice.

"He's here every morning," Janet said. "He never sells anything. Not that I've seen anyway."

Farrell turned and looked at her. She had dressed and was combing her hair. "A cigarette?" he said.

She shook her head. "I don't like them."

"Except when they're marijuana?"

53

She smiled, more relaxed than she had been.

"Not much of that either."

He remembered her baby, her husband, the customs and loyalties that bound her. She had seemed so alone in the water. There were always betrayals in love.

"I'd better be going back soon," she said, folding her towel. "In case Johnny wakes up."

"That's a pity," he said. "So soon. The sun . . . it's so pleasant down here."

"I never stay very long."

He wanted to think that her life was displayed here; mundane, disappointed. The boy on the beach and the sad, hopeless pedlar knew loyalty also. It was never enough. He watched her. A big, baleful sea-gull swooped near them and shrieked. She drew a child's ship on the sand: a big funnel, three portholes, a flag. There was sometimes a cowardice in loyalty, the rhetoric of love. One could go on a long journey backwards to the first small mistake. But her presence denied it. Relaxed, she drew fish on the sand. One wanted to think that one's love offered rescue. This flattery was often the start of affection. She said: "I'm not great in the sun. I burn easily. And Johnny gets frightened without me." The fish had long tails and broad fins and big, wide grinning mouths. She erased one and added an eye to another. They might have been signs in some magic. Her relaxed independence rebuked him. Her loves could be real.

Sweat soaked through his shirt making patches like maps. He scraped through the sand near his feet and discovered a bottle. An insect inside it peered out through the thick, dirty glass. He said: "There's no message," remembering books read in childhood. He had keenly believed in adventure; the islands, the dark pirate's cave and the trees and the treasure. One's childhood was full of escape.

"It would be nice to get one."

As she reached for the bottle he noticed her ring.

"I wonder", he said, "why that pedlar stays down by the sea." He watched, with interest, the old man's slow progress. The voice, melancholy like keening, was getting more faint.

"There's no one down there to buy anything."

"I know that," she said, "but he's always the same."

She polished the bottle with her fingers.

"It's quite old, I think."

The insect fell on to the sand and crawled blindly away.

"There are mice in Señora Perez's house," she said. "But if you say anything about them she calls you a liar. Her cat, that big one, you know, just sits there and looks at them." She held the bottle so that it reflected the sunlight. "It's quite pretty, isn't it? An unusual shape."

He wanted a drink. The old pedlar stood at the edge of the sea, his cloak flapping loosely around his thin ankles. He looked like a tourist's memento, a doll from Morocco. The heat, like a fever, was worse. This would be part of memory; the heat and the insects, her voice and the hot, useless jealousy.

"Perhaps he doesn't really want to sell anything," she said. "He might be . . ." She hesitated. There was no explanation. The man's life was sealed away in some private ritual of loneliness. "A prophet," she said, without conviction, "but then he wouldn't be carrying that tray of stuff, would he?"

"Hardly."

"Farther up the beach," she said, pointing with the bottle, "near the railway line, there's sometimes an old man. He dresses in a brown cloak. He looks like a Franciscan. And he sits there and gathers children around him and chants at them. It sounds weird. David told me he teaches the Koran. I saw him getting cross with them one day when they couldn't chant it back."

"I'd like to see him," Farrell said.

"There are others in the medina almost every evening."

"With children?"

"And adults too. They live like hermits for a while and then come down to the town to teach. Some of them are very old."

55

"Ritual matters," he said, surprising himself. "It's impossible to keep faith without it."

It was ritual that haunted his memories of childhood. One escaped through signs and secret languages into beliefs in other worlds. Fear was avoided and loss made less important. It was a childhood need that never left one, that grew in other ways. Through ritual one kept faith in God, in oneself, in others and in love.

The pedlar walked back along the shoreline, his tray of ornaments seeming to mock him, the leather bags swinging. "I wonder if he cares," Janet said. "I'm sure he does. I'd almost buy something from him." He was strangely unreal. He might have been controlled by wires. One would not have been surprised if he had suddenly shouted and kicked the tray of glittering ornaments into the sea. Farrell remembered a man he had seen in Gibraltar; the self-contained silence and then the shouting, the grotesque dance along the narrow main street, the obscene threats to people who stared.

"Do you think he cares?"

"I wouldn't know," he said evasively. The pedlar walked past a playing child. "Maybe he sells them somewhere else."

"It's difficult to understand." She put on sandals. "I know what you mean by ritual."

The pedlar looked up at them. His sick, fanatical face did not belong on the beach with the children playing, the sound of music from a radio, the pleasure ship moored in a harbour. He stopped and looked at his tray and walked slowly towards them. One could easily imagine menace. His cloak was torn and splashed with blood-like stains.

"I hope he didn't hear us," Janet said. "We'd better buy something from him."

The pedlar bowed jerkily to Farrell. "Taste," he said, squatting on his hunkers before them so that they could see the tray, the metal pendants, the little tinsel brooches. "Taste." He pointed with his finger at a ring. "Taste. Quality." His eyes were bloodshot. One corner of his mouth was almost eaten away by disease. "You want? Or this? No better any-

56

where in the world." His finger trembled as he pointed. He looked across their shoulders, his eyes unblinking. Sweat dripped from beneath his fez. "With these a blessing." His sloping shoulders jerked as he coughed. "A blessing," he repeated.

"Which would you like?"

"I wonder," Janet said. "Are they dear?" she asked the pedlar.

"Dear?"

"The price. Are they cheap? How many dirhams?"

He continued to stare unblinking across their shoulders. "Cheap," he said. "So cheap."

A small drop of pus glistened on the raw, red wound.

"I think maybe this." She picked up a dark metal brooch: a circle surrounding a hand. "I've seen them before."

"The hand of Fatima. A blessing."

"How much is it?" Farrell asked.

The pedlar considered. He looked from the brooch to their faces. Sweat trickled across the bridge of his nose. In a dream, Farrell thought, he would be one's immediate fears, like a hint of impending despair. One so closely avoided these failures.

"Six dirhams."

"You could bargain with him if you like," Janet said.

"It's not worth it."

Farrell gave him the coins.

"They expect it," she said. She pinned the small brooch to her blouse.

"Thank you very much. I like it."

The man stood up. "All right." He walked away without saying anything else, his sandals flopping on the sand.

"I don't see why you should pay for it," she said. "I just thought we should get something from him. You'll let me . . ."

"No. Please. It's only a few shillings anyway. Where's the blessing?"

"I think it's a holy sign. His mouth," she said. "I wonder . . . did you think . . . ? He looked so very ill."

A child ran near to them and laughed.

"Will you wear it?"

"Of course. I like it," she said.

Already, he was afraid of losing her. It was like going back to a place one remembered and fearing that it had changed; a house no longer there, a death, some landmark gone, a friend who had forgotten. There were so many images of loss. One revisited emotion with the same chance of failure.

"Am I keeping you?" he asked.

"No, no. But still, I'd better go now." The child laughed again and they looked around but could see no reason for its amusement. "I enjoyed it a lot," she said.

He looked along the beach. Two men were walking towards the gate. "That man," he said. "Over there." He pointed. "The one in the green shirt. Do you see him?"

"With the pedlar?"

"That's right." The men were crossing the railway line. "I'm certain he's the one who attacked me."

The baby was asleep. A rag doll lay twisted across the blanket, like an accident victim. Señora Perez closed the door. "Abdul!" she called but the cat paid no attention. "Abdul! Como te atreves?" The cat went on up the stairs. Señora Perez followed, fighting against the heat. She killed a bloated cockroach. Three more were fastened tightly against the wall, waiting for the darkness. "Abdul! Abdul, I say!" She paused outside Bannister's door. He had not come in yet. She wiped her forehead and yawned. The heat was like old age; one had to accept new limitations.

"These stairs," she said, looking bitterly back at the cockroaches, the flaking plaster, the shadows. "Madre de Dios!" She hoped that the front door was locked. That man could easily come back. The shadows threatened her like the alien darkness of a place that she had always feared. She blessed herself and climbed, complaining, to the landing outside Farrell's room. The cat was there. She looked at it affectionately. It turned and brushed against her legs. She pushed it away and opened Farrell's door. Sunlight brightened the

58

landing, destroying the shadows, discovering other cockroaches. His suitcase was on the bed.

He could be a bad man, she thought. Suspicion of Traynor returned like a half-healed resentment. She tried the locks of the case. They snapped open; for a moment she feared seeing another pistol. She looked through the clothes, the paperback books and discovered a letter. She read the two pages carefully:

South Hill,
Dartry.
Tuesday.

I got your letter. Is it a joke or am I supposed to take it seriously? A bit of both, I suppose. For a while I didn't intend writing at all and then I thought I would in case you thought it mattered enough to upset me. It only annoyed me. Do you honestly think that I'd want to start all over again as if nothing had happened? Or if that isn't what you had in mind—and I don't really care one way or the other—that I'd just go off with you like that to Gibraltar? Why? So we could reminisce about the good old days. I notice what you say about Darty and the Dropping Well and everything which is all very nice but not really the way that I remember it! It's hardly the time to be sentimental, is it? I'm sure you'll cover the Referendum very well and have a nice time. I'm sure, as well, that I'll continue to have a nice time here. Yes, I'm well, over it completely, it wasn't so bad after all so I'm better than I have been for a long time for various reasons which may not have occurred to you.

Have a nice time,
Catherine.

Who's that? Señora Perez wondered. The small, neat handwriting sloped slightly across the flimsy pages. The cat jumped heavily on to the bed. "Madre de Dios!" She folded the letter and put it back between the books, the packets of cigarettes. She closed the case. This Catherine, she thought, remembering a picture of a tall girl in a white cloak turning her face away from temptation. St. Catherine we implore you, she whispered vaguely as she looked around the room. The door of the wardrobe was open. She could see Traynor's coats; the coloured linings were hanging like bunting as if to celebrate the violence.

The cat left the room before her. She followed it down the stairs. The baby was still asleep. Your father, she thought, is a strange, a very strange man. Up there in the mountains. She had not been out of the town for almost twenty years. Up there nothing good. Bad things happen. Safety rested here between the familiar walls of the house and now even they were threatened. St. Catherine protect us. The kitchen was much too warm, its windows opaque with dust and steam. She felt tired. The letter puzzled her. It started without a greeting.

She opened the front door and looked with hostility at two mountain women carrying bags of fruit. They looked away from her but she could hear them laughing as they went farther down the street. She wished that she had someone to talk to, remembering her husband with an almost forgotten grief. She would go to confession soon; the mumble through the grille had a specially intimate comfort. Forgiveness was a kind of praise.

The cat brushed past her. "Abdul," she called as it moved furtively down the street, afraid of some of the things that she feared. "Abdul, I say it, Abdul!"

A child's voice imitated her and the chant was taken up by others whom she could not see.

"Abdul!" "Abdul!" "Abdul!"

# Chapter Four

Farrell followed them across the town. The man in the green shirt walked quickly, the pedlar half-running by his side. They did not look back. A waiter changing cloths on a café table said something. They stopped and argued with him. Farrell stood in the shadow of an archway. This is pointless, he thought. Their raised voices reached him like snatches of meaningless song.

"Pardon. Pardon."

An old woman came from the archway.

"I'm sorry."

She limped away, bent, like a witch in his childhood; spells cast pains where pins go in, a mumble of evil. Flies crawled across food on a table. The waiter's voice was shrill.

". . . maghzen . . . dahir . . ." He might have been chanting a verse from the Koran. ". . . amoghul . . ." He waved his arms as the pedlar stood impassively silent.

The man in the green shirt replied, his voice quieter, his hand resting on the waiter's shoulder. He looked like a friendly drunk in a bar. Farrell watched them. If they see me, he thought, I can go through this archway. The passage ended at a tall heavily studded, crudely carved door. The waiter brushed crumbs from the table and nodded; it looked like reluctant assent. A man laughed.

It had never before occurred to Farrell that fear could be like this; a growing restlessness, a sense of futility. He wished that he were back on the beach. It made no sense amongst the casual tourists reading lunch-time menus, the girls with bathing suits, the neon signs, the lingering smell of spice. Fear belonged in dark and helpless places; it came scratching at the door. The violence had been real but the growing fear came from the unreality of having no plan. If they see me, he thought, they could follow me easily. Yet, why would they? And what would happen then? The man in the green shirt talked on and the pedlar stared morosely at the trinkets glistening on his tray.

It was not easy to explain an impulse. One's childhood seemed to crowd in on the present, looking for a new experience, clamouring for knowledge. A taxi drove past and the palm trees sighed like pleasure in the breeze. The waiter shrugged his shoulders; he might have been conceding a defeat. He smiled apprehensively at the pedlar, his hand trembling as he took out cigarettes. The smile stayed for too long; like a bad illusion one saw past it to the point of deception. He's afraid, Farrell thought, and saw Susan walking towards him. She was looking suspiciously at the cafés, a guide-book open in her hand. Someone whistled but she paid no attention. She'll see me, he thought, and talk and they'll know that I'm here. This is getting really ridiculous. But the fear throbbed on like a wound.

"What's that?" he heard her asking. "And that?" A woman translated.

"No thanks!"

The man in the green shirt looked around without interest then spoke to the waiter again.

"Just ordinary food. You know, a salad or something?" Her voice had a new note of impatience. "Or fish?"

She might have been explaining a problem to a backward child. The woman laughed cheerfully.

"Feesh! Yes here feesh!"

"Not like that. Grilled."

"Feesh here feesh." The woman's voice rose with enthusiasm.

He remembered her sitting on the deck of the steamer; her innocent loneliness, the slightly old-fashioned clothes. It was only too easy to resent her. She shook her head and came walking towards him again, her trust replaced by an unconcealed impatience. He guessed that her guide-book had let her down; she would feel that as a personal betrayal. He turned and took out cigarettes and lighted one. Her footsteps seemed to falter then she went past. You bitch, he thought, remembering Catherine and the sexual urgency of the drum. The heat was making him feel ill; the cigarette was sticking to his lips. He threw it away and turned. The pedlar's head was visible for a moment in the distance.

I can lose them now, he thought. The beach was like a detailed map of freedom; there were paths away from fear there and paths to love. I can go back now and meet her. An insect droned across his face. Or I can follow them. A passing Arab knocked against his shoulder saying " 'cuse" and smiling awkwardly.

He followed them. The waiter shook the table-cloth, his face intent with concentration. He did not look at Farrell. Meat was cooking on an open spit. The pedlar's head appeared again, elusive, like a target in a shooting-booth. The shoe-shine boys were busy at the café tables. I'm acting like a cub-reporter, Farrell thought, the endless chase to anti-climax. The crowded pavement made his progress slow. He pushed against the crowd. When someone protested he felt a sudden anger. The attack last night became more real, its implications more menacing. The senselessness of violence was continued in this hopeless chase; avoiding being pursued by being the pursuer. He ran and someone cursed, a blur of faces pressing like a dream.

He saw the men and stopped. A flight of steps led towards the Grand Socco. They were near the top, still climbing past the stalls and children playing. The sky, towards which they seemed to climb, was colourless with heat. He thought, like Limbo, wondering why and leaned against the wall. His lungs were sore. His unfamiliar heartbeat slowed a little.

I must have looked ridiculous, he thought, a cartoon figure. The men would soon be out of sight. He climbed some of the steps. The pedlar, silhouetted for a moment, seemed immensely tall, a statue from another way of worship. Then the sky was bare. He hurried up; the tinsmith's stall was made from tattered canvas draped on poles. A little hammer-beat was steady, like a nerve. Grass withered on the sides of steps. The crooked walls of houses were scratched with messages and images of sexual desire. I GOT IT HERE. An arrow pointed towards a step. The English letters were unsteady, sprawling widely like a child's laborious writing.

Near the top, the children watched him, keeping silent. One, a little girl, was carrying a pup. It twisted in her arms and yelped, a sound like loneliness. She held it tighter, staring up at Farrell with some kind of thoughtless scorn. He said "Hello". They did not answer. Then he saw the men going towards the medina. He looked for landmarks from the previous day; on the wall he saw a gate he thought he recognized. "The tower you see is called the Kasbah. It is an ancient prison." A group of tourists straggled slowly past. The fat Moroccan guide talked on without enthusiasm. "The Sultan's palace there and sir, please sir, you listen when I speak. After that this city was what is called an international zone. The French, the German, Spanish . . ." Farrell joined the end of the procession. "Hot," a tall man with sad eyes said. "Wouldn't mind a cup of tea. These places bore me. More or less the same. Last year we went to Greece." His twisted braces held up baggy trousers, white for the occasion. "Didn't spot you in the bus," he said. "The smell is pretty bad."

They walked across the square, the guide's voice droning on about the French. The man in the green shirt looked back then went through the medina gateway. The pedlar followed him.

"Excuse me," Farrell said. The sad eyes watered, "No, no, not at all." A woman offered beads for sale. "I think I'll just see this."

He left the group and went into the medina, past a beggar, on a home-made crutch, who mumbled something at him. Another set of steps led to a narrow street. He ran along it and his footsteps echoed somewhere up above. He turned a corner. Here, the street was hardly wider than a pavement. He walked along past recessed shops and little frontless cafés. Men were eating, crouching on the dirty floors. Alleys led

everywhere, a complicated maze of similarity. He took a turning but found that it led to a doorway. Another doubled back
towards the steps. On braziers, before the cafés, fat meat
burned like oil. People brushed past him. Looking for either
of the men was totally without point. There were too many
streets, too many corners, too many people dressed the same.
He walked on aimlessly and recognized the smell of marijuana.
It was being smoked in cafés. He thought, That bar on the
sea front. They mentioned Traynor there. It was a place to go
to. He tried to remember the context; an old dog near his
suitcase, the angry voice of a man, the waiter boasting "I
could tell you something." He moved on, pushed by the
crowd.

"Yes, another, I think, yes," Bannister said. The waiter
took the glass and asked "With tonic?" Bannister nodded.
The café was much more pleasant than it had been yesterday.
When you had money you could pay for the shade. He
yawned and wondered about Traynor. That fight last night
had been very odd indeed. He wished that Abu were around.
He could ask him straight out. There was something peculiar
going on but he would not get involved. He patted the money
in his pocket and looked contentedly at the street. That old
bitch Señora Perez. She had given him a fright with her talk
about forgetting the letter. If it had not come this would be
an awful day. There were far too many of those. The waiter
came back with the tepid gin and tonic.

"That's fine," Bannister said. "Leave it there. I'll pay you
when I'm going." He scratched the back of his neck. They
were so awkward in the bank, examining the cheque because
he had not got an account there. The same cashier had been
changing it for years yet each time asked for proof of identifica-
tion. They're all the same, he thought, all the same but money
was a most effective bulwark to bitterness. He sipped the gin
and tonic and winced at the thought of the shoe-shine boy.
He must make his allowance last. It was no use having a good
week and then have nothing left for the rest of the month.

E

He needed to plan. His mother had kept detailed household accounts; he could vaguely remember the fat red notebook, the list of items, the prices in her spidery writing. That was forty years ago. A happy birthday, he thought as he sipped the gin. Many happy returns of the day. It was better late than never, like a letter which one has given up hoping to receive. A large car went past towards the European villas on the coastal road. He looked at his watch; it had stopped but it did not matter. There was plenty of time today. He would not buy a picture for another month. That would be his first economy. A little extra money on the side was tempting but it was not worth it in the end. He had been tempted before. Traynor should have known too much to get involved. You couldn't trust these fellows. They were all just crooks dressed up in fancy cloaks. They did not know right from wrong. He watched the women going past. They were like a promise; reminders of the love that all the stars said filled his future.

"Mr. Bannister? My name is Farrell." He looked around, a little startled. "I'm staying with Señora Perez."

"Yes, of course. Of course. Won't you join me for a drink? I wonder how you knew me."

Farrell said, "I saw you yesterday. Coming down the street. I was at my window." He sat down.

"A gin and tonic?"

"Thank you."

"You haven't been here too long, I think?"

"No, only since yesterday."

"A most unfortunate thing that last night," Bannister said, looking for the waiter. "Most unfortunate indeed. I don't believe it's ever happened before." He felt suspicious. Farrell could be a part of whatever was going on. Some instinct warned him to be careful yet he would not mind a talk. The chance of friendship beckoned irresistibly, past the first embarrassment. Farrell was much younger but still . . . "You must dislike poor Traynor," he said jocosely. "Mistaken identity and that . . ." The waiter sauntered over. "Two gins and tonics. It was quite a peaceful house before," he said then hurried on afraid of tactlessness. "An accident, of course. These things can happen anywhere." This little awkwardness was just routine. It happened always with strangers. Like a comic warming up a crowd he wanted to be liked but took no chances. "On the other hand . . ." he said and then forgot what he had meant to say. "The house . . ."

"I think he must have simply been a burglar", Farrell said, "looking for traveller's cheques or money."

"Yes, that's it. A burglar. Almost certainly."

He felt a little dizzy from the gin. "That's almost certainly it," he said without conviction. "Lots of thieves around. The whole damn place." He guessed that Farrell could not yet be thirty. At that age he had still known galaxies of hope.

"You've been here quite some time?"

"Some time."

He saw no reason to be more explicit.

"It suits me very well," he said.

The gin arrived. The waiter's thumbs had left a trellis on the glasses.

"I hope it's to your taste."

"It's very good. I wonder", Farrell said, "if the thief, whoever he was, could have mistaken me for this Mr. Traynor. Mistaken identity as you said yourself. You're a friend of Traynor's, I believe."

"Oh no, no," Bannister said quickly. "No. Not a friend. A mere acquaintance you could say. We're on nodding terms. Occasional drinks and that. I'm sure you know the way it is yourself. Two fellow countrymen in a foreign place. Our both being British is a kind of bond but nothing more than that."

It's very odd, he thought. Who told him that we were friends? It sounded like a kind of threat; a voice at a seance that claimed some kinship. Why should he be asking me questions?

"What made you think", he asked, trying to sound bland, "that that might be the case. You're not at all like Traynor. He's a taller man, much older. Not at all like you."

67

Sweat had made his collar damp. He put a finger to his tie; like a talisman, its well-tied knot brought thoughts of reassurance. "I should think", he said jocosely, "that old Traynor would be rather flattered."

Farrell smiled. "It was only a thought," he said. "You suggested it yourself. It must have been a thief. And yet there's something strange."

New apprehension moved through Bannister's mind. It was not bloody fair; the day his cheque arrived, the day he made his plans. The small jocosities all drained away like trust. He felt a little frightened.

"I dislike the heat," he said, putting his hands upon the table. "I prefer the evening. Then you have a breeze down by the harbour." It was clumsy but it seemed to work.

"It can be tiring," Farrell said.

"Except in winter. Then it's very pleasant here, of course." He took a sip of gin and stared morosely at the sky. "I sometimes wish for rain," he said. "My mother liked it, I believe. I don't know why I think that yet I seem to feel she told me once. You probably know that kind of feeling. Odd experience."

"Does Mr. Traynor work at anything?"

"No. I don't know of a job. Perhaps", he said, "like me he has a source of independent means."

Farrell offered him a drink.

"I really shouldn't," Bannister said. "You're here on holiday?"

"Yes."

The terseness of the answer was surprising. Gulls called harshly from the hills behind the town. A small policeman dressed in baggy khaki uniform walked past, muttering to himself as if rehearsing evidence.

"For a short while," Farrell said. "I might move down to Casablanca. Have you been there?"

"No, no, no. I haven't actually left Tangier. The climate," he said, "according to accounts is very hot. Much worse than here. It wouldn't suit me at all. I don't mind warmth but anything more than that . . . It's constitutional, I suppose, whatever you're used to . . ."

This blustering, he thought, is an inevitable part of life; the woman dressing, clerks in banks and boys; waiting for the day to end and for hope to start again. He understood his fear. The years had brought some recognition of a fundamental truth. The imperatives one found for life were mostly ones of safety. The ordered day, anticipated moves, predicted feelings; from these alone one found a simple reason to continue. Causes disappeared like tears. They were not worth it. There was nothing left but hope and, in the daylight, an insistence on routine, one's own attempt, however bad, at finding meaning. Watching Farrell order drinks, he thought, a threat is like a voice that comes from nowhere, saying something trivial. Love was like a threat; a voice, a woman's body moving in the dark, the smell of sweat, a brief conviction that one's life could change. It never did, of course. And yet one chased that threat, abandoned safety, jerked helplessly, lay limp, believing love would come and forge a new routine. It was the promise; walking streets and having drinks, one waited, facing disappointment, counting time.

"If you don't mind the heat," he said, "I'm sure you'll like it in Casablanca. People tell me it's unusual. A peculiar kind of place."

"I've heard that too."

"And Marrakesh, of course, they say is nice as well. A very pleasant town. The Bahia Palace . . ."

He had read about it somewhere. Conversation was made up of flotsam, washed up, gathered carefully, presented like a truce. His head was tingling from the heat. The small policeman walked back down the street, his hands behind his back, still giving evidence. The gin seemed cooler. Insects curled like smoke around the table.

"I envy you your freedom", Farrell said, "to sit here in the sun. Or move on if you like."

He doesn't mean it, Bannister knew. One found a gift for seeing falsehood after years of loud, false welcomes, drunken declarations, lies. He touched his tie-knot and smiled vaguely. He's still asking questions, he thought. Nosey. You've got to be on your guard.

"Your health," he said.

The glass was warm and sticky in his hand. The gin reflected light and glistened like a little crystal ball. That day in Blackpool, in a stuffy tent. "I see three girls, two boys. A joy to both of you." The rain had seeped right through his shabby suit.

"I'm glad that I met you," Farrell said. He had a way of speaking quickly as if accusations lay behind the friendly, harmless words. His face was slightly burned, skin peeling from his forehead and his cheeks.

Bannister noticed that he did not seem at ease. He knew the signs and wondered how they could be used to his advantage.

"Mrs. Merton," Farrell said, "who stays at Señora Perez's house. Her husband's away, I believe."

"I believe he is," Bannister said. "I haven't seen him for some while." This scent was leading somewhere; eagerly he followed his advantage. "You're a friend of Mrs. Merton's then?"

"No. I met her for the first time today."

"You knew her husband perhaps?"

Some gin slopped from his glass and stained his trousers. Cool, he thought, be cool, you could be on to something here remembering Janet passing on the stairs, the long pink dressing gown. She likes me.

"No, I only wondered," Farrell said. "He's not away with Traynor is he?"

"Not that I know."

"Is he much older than her?"

"Hardly," Bannister said. Farrell's impatience pleased him. This was like the game one sometimes played and almost always lost. The way that she cried at night would be a certain point of interest but he held it back, anticipating moves, keeping advantage. One could gamble with another's interest

70

when the stakes were as low as this. The tingling heat became more bearable. He said, "They're both so young." The phrase was false. He wondered where he could have heard it used before. "A student type," he said. He knew that this was worthless information. Farrell looked away.

"I've just come down from the medina," he said. "Do you know your way around? It's like a maze, isn't it? I wonder if it's possible to get to know it well? To sort out one street from the other?"

"Quite impossible," Bannister said. He realized that he was slightly drunk.

Farrell finished his drink. "Still, you must know it well," he said, "having been here for some while?"

"Some streets, some parts. One tends to stick to what one knows."

"There's a bar near the harbour. I can't remember its name. It's quite a small one," Farrell said. "The barman is English. You wouldn't know it I suppose?"

"I'm afraid I don't," Bannister said. He yawned. "Excuse me. Does this bar interest you in some way?"

"Not really. I just wondered if it were popular. I happened to have a drink there yesterday. I'd better move on now. I've one or two things to do." He stood up. "It's nice to have met you. I'm sure we'll run into each other again."

"I'm sure we will."

Bannister watched him walk away. I wouldn't trust him, he thought, too many questions. But he hadn't given anything away. The waiter came to the table, collecting glasses.

"Another."

He felt obscurely uneasy.

Janet dislike the evenings most. The shadows deepened and a cockroach crawled across the unpolished floor. She moved around the room, afraid of waking Johnny, touching the things she owned; a book, a comb, the coat that she had bought in London. The silence went on like a noise. It was too hot to sleep and too early. Yet there was nothing else to do. The books were read, their pages brittle and mis-shapen from the heat. She saw the cockroach and killed it carefully; its body cracked like a nut at Hallowe'en. Another whirred in some dark corner and she shivered.

"Do you love me?" she whispered to Johnny.

The optimistic question seemed to come back like an echo, staying in the air, unanswered. She went closer to his cot. His breathing changed, became a little cry, then became calm again. "You love me, don't you?" It was ludicrous to think of him being cruel and yet his silence seemed so wanton. Sleep was sometimes love's revenge. He stirred and clenched one fist. It might have been a dream, an adult awareness of the tension. Dreams were memories put right with new perspectives. One believed in them. They seemed to hold the truth, admitting fears and flaws that daylight kept away. They were, she supposed, one's conscience; like a child examining sins before the ordeal of confession one examined them for details of despair. One faced the truth as penance. "Don't you love me?" This was like the time that dragged on through an illness, nothing happening, a contracted world, dust upon a broken chair. She touched his head. He *was* like David. One imagined it then saw it in a smile, a way of staring. These were ever-present images of love, dislike and loss; the casual gesture broken like a code and read, the changing moods, the silent struggle for survival.

Bannister, moving around in his room, broke the silence. Creaking floorboards were a chart to his position; at the window, near the door, back to the window again. He might have been a restless passenger totting up a mile in a ship's small cabin. She watched the ceiling as if, cartoon like, his feet would soon come through. The footsteps went on like an obsession, creaking restlessness and boredom through the house. She wondered what he thought about. The creaking stopped. She heard his coughing and then the creaking began again. It was even worse than the silence. David used to swear up at the sound. She saw the narrow face, the humour that too easily grew sour.

72

Her towel was hanging from the window. Like a flag, she thought; the photographs of monarchs on a balcony came aimlessly to mind. The small, bored faces and the arms upheld, the fairy-story's end. She took it in. The street was empty. Clouds were flexing like a muscle in the darkening sky. The footsteps stopped and bedsprings creaked. At last, she thought, I hope he's there for good but she knew that it would start again. She lay down on the bed. The cover seemed to trap some source of coolness. Two more hours, she thought, before undressing, getting into bed, a pill to help her sleep. The clock was stopped. She thought vaguely about Farrell. It was puzzling how he had left her on the beach and chased that pedlar. The small brooch was on the table. Johnny stirred again and seemed to whisper like someone at prayer. She closed her eyes; the pedlar, Farrell smiling, watching her. A journalist. She thought, When David comes back it will be the way it was; the laughter turning quickly into tears.

The evening grew a little noisier; some music from a bar, a voice inquiring for directions, laughter from another street. Down near the beach the night-club signs would be switched on, the girls would move through bored routines, their bodies brown with oil. She missed the laughter. Broken promises were littered through the days since love was real. She thought again of Farrell, watching her. The sea had been so cool; the man, the boy, the pedlar, brooches glistening brightly on a tray.

The knock was hesitant. She watched the door. The handle turned and someone knocked again.

# Chapter Five

A small sound, like the chewing of a mouse, came from behind him. Traynor looked around unwillingly. It was very dark. A line of light between the shutters of a distant window seemed miraculous; a fiery sword, salvation. Traynor cleared his throat. "Hello," he said, dreading an answer. "Who's there?" His voice came out distorted, sounding like a moan. "Hello."

The alley stretched back towards the mosque. The dark disintegrated there and formed into tall shadows of a porch, some steps, a door. "Who's there?" The sound had stopped. He cleared his throat again. "Durcan?" he said and for a moment feared that it might be. "Durcan?" He leaned against a wall. It crumbled near his head and dust fell down inside his collar. "Damn!" It itched against his shoulders like mosquitoes. While he scratched himself he peered across the darkness, looking for a moving shape. The sound went on. He guessed that it was a mouse, intent on some small destruction. "Hello?" he said then, satisfied, went down the alley towards the deeper darkness. Round this way, he thought, but when he turned the corner nothing was familiar. Rotting fruit had been thrown across the uneven cobbles of the lane. Its sourness filled him with revulsion. There should be another turning here, bricks jutting, a passage to the right. He felt along the wall. A spider crawled on to his hand. He killed it, swearing, and heard voices coming through the wall. They seemed like an argument, then a burst of laughter, then the argument again. A family, he thought, up late. He had put the pistol back into his pocket. As he felt the butt his face began to twitch out of control. He checked the safety-catch. The fruit, he thought, was like a damaged body, rotting useless and alone between the trenches. There were

74

private wars that one fought; the trenches changed, the ammunition was of a different kind. The wars were waged in offices and parks and in cobbled lanes. One fought against dismissal, sniped at discovery, alone, like something lying near the trenches. The rules were never the same. The only victory was postponement of defeat. One's little weaknesses were posted up for scrutiny. "Nine previous charges of a similar nature. Asks that these be taken into consideration." All one's suffering could be paraphrased as dismally as that.

His fingers scraped across the barrel of the pistol. It was slightly rusty. Oil, he thought, it should be oiled. He had bought it on the Edgware Road. No questions had been asked. The weapons changed as one grew older; they were more conventional and safe. One looked for privacy and guarded it as if it were one's youth. The bugles blew across the wilderness of choice.

If the turning isn't here, he thought, it must be farther down. He went along the lane, feeling the wall like a guide-rope. There was something here. A courtyard gate. He heard a voice, the rattle of some glasses. In the darkness, smells seemed stronger; mint and oil, the rotting fruit. A dog went limping past, ignoring him. Unusual, he thought, watching the shape. His fingers brushed across the doorway while his other hand stayed tight around the pistol.

"Harry?"

Traynor stopped. Two men were sitting in the lane, their backs against the courtyard wall. The glow of a cigarette showed their position. Durcan, Traynor thought. He pressed against the wall. The glow intensified and showed their shapes, their feet across the lane, their shadowed faces. Both were wearing cloaks. He cleared his throat; a moment from the war. The pistol kept him calm. He held it firmly, staring at the shapes. To go back now would be a greater risk. They were certain to know these lanes. Strategic wisdoms came back to his mind. Keep the enemy in sight. His face was twitching but he still felt very calm.

"Harry," one of them said. "Need help, Harry?"

It was not Durcan. They were Arabs, he saw, as the cigarette flared again.

"I amn't Harry."

It sounded feeble. They laughed and Traynor took the pistol from his pocket. The safety-catch was on.

"What your name, Harry?"

"Now look here," Traynor said. He felt sweat gather near his moustache.

"If you're looking for trouble . . ."

"No trouble."

The man's voice was only a little louder than a whisper. Traynor said, "What do you want?"

"What you want, Harry?"

He thought, They call *everyone* Harry. It's pure coincidence. Pimps. He moved away from the wall. The men stood up and came towards him. "Stay where you are," he said. His voice was shaking. This surprised him. I'm calm, he thought, I'm in control. One held on to military standards, the belief in absolute precision. But the rules were entirely different now.

"Just stay where you are," he said.

The men had stopped. He released the safety-catch.

"No, wait now minute, Harry."

"Just stay where you are."

He had not used the pistol before but the small Italian had reassured him. An excellent gun, sir. Feel it. Lift. A bargain. He pointed it at the taller of the men.

"If you move any nearer," he said, "I'll shoot."

"We didn't do anything, Harry."

"I said to stay where you are."

I must, he thought, be near the gate. At the end of this lane there's a turning that leads to the steps. If I find it I can get to Bannister. A light went on in a narrow window. He could see the shape of the lamp. His facial twitch embarrassed him. A man was judged by levels of composure. In the army he had failed to pass the most important tests.

"Harry?"

He wondered what to do. They blocked his path. He dare not turn back. He said, "Do you know Durcan?"

"Duckin? Duckin, Harry?"

"Durcan," he said. "Do you or don't you?"

He felt almost certain that they were bluffing. They were Durcan's men all right, not pimps or beggars waiting in the darkness. Yet they could not have known that he would come this way. It had been entirely accidental. He doubted if Durcan even knew that he was in Tangier. The days of hiding lay behind him like a criminal record. One of the men said "Harry" and moved nearer.

"Stop."

I'll shoot, he thought. They're forcing me. Sweat ran into his eyes and burned like salt. One made decisions this way, unaware of options.

"If you let us to pass."

"Stay back."

His hands were shaking. If I shoot, he thought, the sound will be appalling. It was loneliness that moved him most, not fear. He felt betrayed by nerves as he tried to stop his hands from shaking. Courage was the quality one sought. He leaned against the wall. The sour smell of decay came from behind him like a memory of death. He was exhausted and an open sore was throbbing on his foot.

"We pass, Harry."

"You're Durcan's men," he said. "I know. I'm not a bloody fool." He could not see their faces. The smaller man said, "Dickin. No." His voice sounded unusually high.

The tiredness and loneliness, the days of hiding, all gathered in him like a poison. One lived on for death; the journey was not worth it. In an alley or a battlefield one faced the same decisions made by other men. Life was accidental. Still, he thought, the standards, there are bluffs and knew that fear was coming like a local fever, unexpectedly. He thought, This hesitation is a weakness. They'll be armed. He longed for the comfort of a whisky.

"Why wrong, Harry?"

"Turn around," he said.

They did not move.

"You'd better turn around. Bastards!" he shouted.

"Listen, Harry. No we."

"Turn around I said."

The taller man shrugged.

"What you say."

They turned.

"Fool Harry."

"You're the bloody fools," he said.

"Shit."

"I'm armed."

There always was a boast, a way of gaining victory, or so one told oneself. One grew more used to loss, the opportunities squandered.

"Move," he said. "Move towards the gate. I'll follow."

"No gate."

"You know the gate. Move now. Don't act the fool."

When we get there, he thought, I'll think of something else. The men walked slowly forward, their sandals scratching on the lane in what might have been deliberate provocation. Ignore it, he thought. He shook the pistol. "Quieter." They changed the pace of their steps. He squeezed the trigger a little and immediately felt more calm. He was in control. It could turn out very well. Durcan's men would know some useful things. The money in his pocket was an unexpected future.

They walked like mourners, acting out a grief, the heavy steps, the sloping shoulders. If he recognized a turning . . . but in the darkness they all seemed the same.

"To the gate," he said.

"No gate."

Authority was something that he admired. It was always manly. It was there in accents, gestures, ways of taking other men for granted. If he found it now these last weeks could be worth while.

The taller man moved quickly, turning, jumping forward with a knife and Traynor squeezed the trigger.

The sound was not as bad as he had expected. The shriek was louder. As the man fell to his knees the knife hit Traynor's shoe. The shriek went on; it echoed from the walls. Traynor moved back a step. Even when the man lay silent one seemed to hear his pain.

"No Dickin, boss," the smaller man implored across his friend's body. "Never. Come here from Tetuan." Traynor believed him. He could not see any blood but it must be there, seeping in the darkness.

"Jesus," he said. "I didn't want to shoot. He forced me. He forced me with the knife. It was self-protection. You saw that. Why did he force me? The stupid bastard forced me. You saw . . ."

The man ran down the lane.

"Come back! Jesus, you witnessed. You must tell them the truth."

After a few moments he could not hear the sound of running any more but there was excited shouting from near by. He stuffed the pistol back into his pocket. There's a gate near here, he thought. It's over there somewhere to the right. He stepped across the body and left it there, discarded, like the fruit.

# Chapter Six

Farrell saw that she was crying. He said, solicitously, "Janet".
She shook her head and went on crying quietly. The tears
had left a track beneath her eyes. Make-up spread like a dis-
figurement across her cheeks. He said, "I'm sorry if I said
. . ." She shook her head again. It was almost as if she had
been interrogated. She sat across from him in the same blouse
and jeans, her long legs stretched forward, the red night-light
throwing a shadow on her shoulder. The baby was asleep.
Outside the window, darkness was gathered like a hostile force.

"I can't remember . . ." he said.

"No," she said. "It's only foolish. Don't mind. It's nothing
that you said."

She tried to smile. A tear had caught on her lip. She licked
it away and smiled at him like a child, her eyes glistening
brightly.

"If I had a handkerchief," he said, "I'd give it to you. I
never have one when I should."

"I have one here, I think."

She went to the bedside table and searched through
clothes, some books, knocking a phial of pills. "Here it is,"
she said. "I knew."

He watched as she wiped her eyes. "I don't know what
you'll think," she said. "So sudden. I hate it. I must look like
a fool."

"I'm sorry that you're upset."

"But that's just the thing," she said. "I'm not."

She sat down again. The shadow moved from her shoulder
to the side of her face and stayed there, looking like blood.
"I'll make up in a minute," she said, "when I'm sure that I'm
finished." She smiled, so matter of fact that she might have
been an actress in an old familiar part.

"There's no sign of tears," he said, lying, because he wanted to help her restore the conversation and break this tension. She pulled the handkerchief tight between her fingers. "It must be your eyesight," she said. "I'm sure there's bound to be signs. Could we talk more quietly now. In case we wake Johnny. He's such a good sleeper, isn't he?"

Farrell nodded. The baby lay there like a warning, a huge inhibition. Its breathing went on like a subtle reminder of pacts and of promises made; love sworn between others. He said, "He's a quiet child," unsure of the praise that was wanted. "He's like you." She twisted the handkerchief tightly and looked towards the window.

"You think so?"

"A little," he said.

"I can't see it."

He regretted the comment. One blundered too easily that way. A large, wide-winged moth knocked again and again against the night-light. Its shadow appeared on the wall, vast and threatening. Janet said, "Aren't they awful? Compared with the ones back at home. They're so horribly big."

This tenuous link, a shared city, was almost as good as a mutual friend. She made up, leaning close to the mirror. He watched her movements carefully. There were damp patches on her blouse. The worn blue corduroy jeans clenched tightly around her buttocks. "I'm sorry", she said, "and embarrassed. I don't often cry like that. It means nothing. Except that I'm tired, I suppose." She combed back her hair.

"I'll go soon. I know that I'm keeping you up."

"No you're not," she said, leaving the comb on the table. "I'm always up late anyway. Please don't go until you want to."

She leaned over the baby. "Poor, poor little fellow," she said.

Farrell crushed out a cigarette in the saucer near his chair.

"I wish I had a drink for you," she said. "I used to have whisky but it's all gone. I think Señora Perez drank some. She does get drunk sometimes, you know." She sat down on the bed. "I saw her drunk one evening in the kitchen, doing a dance. I don't think that she remembers. I never mentioned it to her."

"Is her husband dead?"

"I suppose so. She never talks about him anyway. And there aren't any pictures around. I suppose", she said, after a moment, "that there *was* a Señor Perez. Maybe she invented him. And bought a ring in the market. I wouldn't be at all surprised."

The theory seemed to please her. She lay back, her shoulders resting against the wall. The moth hit the lamp loudly and fell, like a withered leaf, to the floor. She grimaced. "They frightened me at first," she said. "And the cockroaches. It really is a horrible house. Did you ever see the Arab houses? They're so much nicer in comparison. Rooms around a courtyard. And they spend a lot of time on the roofs. It must be so cool and clean except, I suppose, in the very poor ones. David tried to rent one but he couldn't. They wanted some impossible rent."

She's trying to cover her embarrassment, Farrell thought with a detachment that came from Catherine's crying. In a minute she could be nervous again and start to cry. Unless I say the right thing. The detachment remained intact and ready for use like a skill that he had acquired.

"Don't you find your room very stuffy?" Janet asked. "At night? And in the morning?"

"Very."

"If it weren't for the swimming I'd melt. I don't know how Johnny is so good. The poor little fellow must feel it."

He said, "I'm sorry that I left you on the beach." She looked at him, surprised, as if unable to think of a casual answer. She sat up, away from the wall and said, "You looked so funny on the beach. Skulking after them like a detective!"

They had been speaking in this easy way before she had started suddenly to cry. He looked across at her and saw that there were still some marks from the tears beneath her eyes. They gave her an expression of weariness. She looked like a woman at the end of some impossible vigil.

"Have I smudges left?"

"Not at all."

"I know that I have," she said. "The light is so bad. And I've almost run out of make-up." She crossed her legs. The bed creaked a little as she moved her arms around to support herself. "I've been meaning to go to the chemist. There's a nice one down near the beach."

There was no sign of nervousness now. The fact that she had cried seemed of little importance. There was no need for detachment. He lighted a cigarette and said, half-seriously, "I thought you'd be impressed that I wanted to catch the thief."

"But that poor old pedlar," she said. "He's there every morning. I've seen him a hundred times. I honestly think that he's the most harmless man in Tangier."

"He may be but that other fellow . . ."

"The man in the green shirt?"

She refused to take it seriously.

"I'm almost certain . . ." he said.

"I know," she said. "You're certain it was he . . ."

". . . who attacked me last night."

They laughed.

"If you had the bump," he said.

The baby gasped and turned in the cot and they watched but he did not wake. One could invent one's own inhibitions, Farrell thought, yet there were areas of pride and of possessiveness that grew more real than love. He felt desire for her; her body posing casually on the bed betrayed the feelings she might have, the loves and loyalties.

"I hope it doesn't hurt much now," she said.

"Do you really? It's almost better."

The desire was unreliable, he knew, a trick that worked or failed with knowledge. Susan had prompted it with faint hostility, offering nothing more than a brief experience that was not new. One looked back at the past, the long monotony of other pointless lusts, suspicious of one's disappointments, often angry at one's needs.

"I bet you'll lock your door tonight?"

"Is there a lock?" he asked.

He wondered if he understood her crying. Premonitions of involvement would cut deeply through a world; a baby sleeping, lonely nights that brought their own kind of security. One at least found independence, hoping less, relying more on one's acceptance of a system of betrayal. This view if found in sadness was, he thought, a lot to risk; to go once more to hope then back to disappointment.

But that was Catherine's letter. Janet sat there, vague, elusive. Other men and griefs had shaped her hopes and caused her sudden tears. There was no way of knowing what she thought. He shrank away from questions that were answers to unspoken questions she might like to ask. Admitting jealousy was easy when desire was satisfied. The obscure furniture had gathered bulk within the growing darkness. Like a cage, the cot imprisoned hope and failure. Catherine's tears were choices she had made. He thought, I have her letter still, and wondered why he had brought it, why it had not been destroyed. He had re-read it often in Gibraltar, feeling very little.

"Do you like your baby?" he asked.

The question lay between them like a weapon; either one could use it.

"How do you mean?" she said.

Tobacco smoke curled slowly around the light. A cockroach whirred in a corner and Farrell remembered Catherine's face distinctly.

"It's a silly question," he said. "Forget that I asked it."

"No, tell me. What did you mean?"

"I suppose I wondered if you could go on loving someone who doesn't love you back. I'm sure it's as trite as that."

"You mean that Johnny doesn't love me?"

"Well hardly," Farrell said, aware of how ridiculous it was.

"I mean he hasn't got any choice, has he? Or any real alternative. And neither have you. That can hardly be love."

"But of course it can," she said. "You don't just make cool choices."

"I do."

"No you don't! It isn't at all like that."

"Then you believe", he said, "in predestination."

"What on earth has that got to do with it?"

"Somewhere", he said, "there has got to be a real assent of the will. If there isn't then love and almost everything else is quite ridiculous. And violent."

"I made that assent," she said, smiling in a way that annoyed him.

"Maybe you did," he said. "Or maybe you just think you did. You may be quite expert for all I know, at self-deception. But he didn't. The baby."

"Existence is a kind of assent," she said. "He trusts me. Is it possible to have trust without love?"

"Completely possible, I would have thought."

"But not love without trust?"

"Ideally no," he said. "But I imagine it's rather common, don't you?"

She shook her head. I only want to hurt her, he thought, I want to take her faith away. If I could simply admit that I'm jealous. She watched the cot as if it were an altar. That was the way that one prayed, trusting in a love that one hadn't even asked for, praying to an absent God. It was even possible to picture God like that; a huge demanding baby, making its presence bearable by someone's promise that it really cared. A God who did not care would soon destroy belief and be ignored. He said, "I don't know why I started such a pointless conversation."

"I don't think it's entirely pointless."

"You must. A baby is simple to you. You love it and it loves you back. When I don't understand things I invariably complicate them. I'm sorry for doing it now."

"It's not difficult to love him," she said. "He's mine. But

85

it's not exactly simple either. It's hard to explain. He *depends* on me, remember."

"And that's a burden."

"Do you think so?"

"Sometimes."

"Sometimes I think so too," she said. "I suppose it's getting rather late."

He stood up, resentfully.

"I'm sorry to have kept you up."

"No you didn't," she said. "I was glad of the company. It gets a bit lonely here sometimes. David will be coming back soon. I think we'll go to Paris then. I hope so. He's writing a book about customs in other societies and how we've adapted them in our own. The things we've inherited." She stood up and leaned against the wall. "Like pagan places in Ireland becoming holy wells."

"That might be interesting."

"I think it will. He's done quite a lot of research into the old mythologies. The Christ and Muhammad figures who were there before Christ and Muhammad. Red Indian Incarnations and that kind of thing."

The cockroach whirred again, a small, insistent threat from out of the darkness. She went to the cot and looked down at the baby.

"I wouldn't mind meeting him," Farrell said.

"David? You must."

Her reaction was disappointing. He thought, It's unconventional to be here yet all the awkwardness defined a new convention. Like a barrier or a secret charm the baby kept her safe. She moved around the cot, preoccupied with duties. There was innocence in faithfulness. It saddened him; he should not have risked hurting her.

"He should find some new mythologies here," he said. The bitterness in his voice was like hostility. She stared at him and he tried to cover up. "Another way of life," he said but he knew that she was not fooled. Her shadowed face seemed quite expressionless. They might have had no conversation.

They stood like strangers staring awkwardly across a waiting-room.

"You don't like the sound of the book?"

"Of course I do."

"There's no reason why you should."

"Or why I shouldn't," he said. "It's been done before but your husband's approach could be new. It's a question of freshness," he said without conviction. "I didn't mean to sound dismissive."

"You didn't. Just bored."

"With what?"

She moved from the shadow and shrugged as if resisting a challenge.

"Books about mythology, maybe. Or me."

"I'm interested in both," he said.

"I want it to be a good book," she said. "It's very important to him. He hoped to get a new grant. If it turns out well."

He was relieved by her relaxation. She smiled so openly that the stirrings of sadness returned.

"He's taken so many notes," she said. "In about a dozen different notebooks." She spoke with a certain complacency as if ignoring all possible points of contention.

"I can imagine the work," he said but what he could imagine was the waste; the absences, tenuous acts of faith and acts of doubt in another's ability to love. The deceptions one learned to practise, the attempts to charm or lie or flatter were faithless. The madman shouting in Gibraltar had called on God to witness his new-found freedom. The claim had made sense to Farrell. It announced the end of deception and the chances of being deceived.

"Keep away from the man in the green shirt," she said. He opened the door.

"I'll find him."

He wanted to ask, "Are you happy?" The heat in the passage smelled sour. Someone was talking in Bannister's room. He blamed the baby again for his inhibition and saw, with a gratitude that pained him, that she was smiling.

87

"I'll see you tomorrow," he said.

She nodded. Passing by Bannister's room he heard the unfamiliar worried voice. "But I wouldn't ask you, would I, if it weren't absolutely necessary to me?"

He went on up to his room.

# Chapter Seven

He ran along the alley, stumbling through a pile of rotting rubbish. The smell persued him; something stuck to his shoes and stayed there like evidence of guilt. The pistol jogged in his pocket. "Oh Jesus Christ!" The pain in his side grew sharper. A bullet could be no worse, he thought, as he turned a corner and ran into farther darkness. He could not hear the voices any more. He stopped for a moment and waited for the pain to ease; he had to bend down to breathe. The pistol pressed against his stomach. A shape near by jerked suddenly. The hopeless, tubercular cough cut sharply through the darkness. Traynor watched the shape with horror. It moved from side to side and the cough went on. There were so many kinds of death. One could not face them all with courage; alone in the darkness one heard the cry and the cough. He may not be dead, I saw no blood, he thought. If they weren't Durcan's men they still weren't up to anything good. Why did he turn with the knife? The shape spat noisily. The germs, he thought, are everywhere. I don't believe that he wasn't Durcan's man. The shape had human features; legs bent awkwardly, an arm supporting weight. It coughed hopelessly again. The body back there somewhere might be coughing also, Traynor thought. He did not want it to be dead. The other man could still give evidence. I spend too much time by myself, he thought. It seemed to matter now. Reproachfully he looked back at failed leadership. The first mistakes were fatal. After those one followed courses without choice. He went on past the shape. The man—his face was visible now—spat noisily and Traynor winced as if contamination could not be avoided. Perhaps it can't, he thought, in three years' time, I might be coughing too because he spat as I was passing by. It sometimes took as long as that to find that harm had been done. Things changed; forgotten enemies gained power and paid old scores.

He heard the shouting then. They're coming close, he thought, they must have heard me running. He turned. "The gate. The arch," he said. "Where is it?" He tried to show an arch, bending his fingers together, leaning close to the man. "To the Socco. How do I get to the Socco? Where is the gate? Tell me." His voice was louder than he had intended. "Tell me. You know what I'm saying. The gate."

The man shook his head.

"Of course you know the gate. Don't act the bloody fool. Money," he said, pulling some coins from his pocket. "Look money. The gate, where's the gate?"

The man scratched his nose then pointed vaguely into the darkness before starting to cough again. Traynor threw the coins to the ground. "Down that way?" he asked. The shouting was coming from much nearer. He said, "Is it far?" Tears ran down the old man's face; he brushed them away with his knuckles and stared up at Traynor. His face was still twisted from coughing. His hand shook. He mumbled something and watched as if intent on gaining approval.

"Maybe you don't know," Traynor said sadly. "Maybe you don't!" He felt so helplessly trapped that conversation seemed imperative. "They're coming near but if I run I could be running towards them, you see. The sounds are all wrong in here. You'd wonder what's the point."

The man stared up at him anxiously. He held one hand against his ragged chest as if a bullet had torn it apart. His obsequious eyes glistened with tears. He muttered, pointing at the ground and Traynor swore. "You stupid bastard!" For a moment he was tempted to hit out; his fist would strike that face with something like authority. He turned and ran. The man coughed harshly. It might have been a curse cast angrily through the darkness. Shadows moved like bodies, writhing in the agony of death. I'll shoot again, he thought. They won't come near me. He had some bullets in his pocket. In the alleyways his running released echoes. Sounds came back, confused, like memories of war. The smells had been worst, his memory sometimes prompted, smells of rotting fruit, of wounds unwrapped in makeshift hospitals, of bodies sick with fear. The sounds had not been so bad; they brought a sense of action which, however pointless, seemed to guarantee that there would have to be an end. The waiting hinted at a kind of immortality.

He ran down narrow steps and saw the gate of the medina. In the distance, pilgrims' fires were burning, comforting and free. The sky was luminous. A bat flapped from the darkness of the wall and squealed as if in pain; its graceless wings were skeletal and smudged. "Get off there!" Traynor said and watched, remembering childhood lore of wings being caught in hair. He felt the pistol-handle; shrieks inside the trenches, vomit, one man's face cut open. This is fear, he thought, ashamed. The bat was out of sight. Some instruments wailed plaintively from where the fires were. It was friendly there but baleful near the gate. The fear of knives was worst, the little cuts that stretched across the stomach. He had heard of that and other tortures, all precise and unimproved by centuries of use. One lived within decay and breathed it; the stench of death was everywhere. He thought, They haven't followed me, and listened. There were no sounds from the lanes. Perhaps they've only found the body now. The eerie silence threatened him with unexpected action. The atrocities were smaller now but no less cruel or real. It wasn't called a war. The rules had changed. One fought without a plan. The piping went on, a lament for something changed or lost or dead and shadows moved across the flicker of the fires.

He stepped unwillingly away from near the gate and walked across the square. The open vulnerability of the action made him tremble. Knives came silently, he thought. That's nonsense. No one throws a knife. Not here. One's nerves retained some memories of their own. One flinched away from things that had been encountered as if knowledge or experience had taught one what to fear. If there were times for trust he had not come across them.

Self-defence, he thought, it was a simple case of self-defence, the knife, the man about to spring and Durcan's orders. He was not at fault. The other man had witnessed that. "Jesus Christ," he whispered. He heard the shouting and the music stopped. I'm nearly there, he thought. He ran across the open space and down a flight of steps to a street.

"Sex, Tommy. Sex with me."

The woman pulled a veil away and smiled at him. She used a pocket-torch to light her face. Some of her teeth were broken. "Very good in bed. The French way. Suck it if you want."

She's not very young, he thought. Her face retained a kind of spurious youth. The young were arrogant. They had what he so very much desired. He saw them on the beaches, boasting with their arrogant bodies. They would have no fear of dreams. My wife was very beautiful, he thought. So very beautiful. Beautiful and boastful like a symbol of one's wealth. He put his fingers to his forehead and felt the sweat. The woman smiled again. "How much?" he asked, an automatic question. The money was in his pocket. He could feel the thick wad of notes. They seemed as heavy as the pistol.

"No. Not much," she said. "Good value. Show you things." She took his arm. "My room it is near."

I wonder why they haven't followed me, he thought. Her fingers fussed around a button on his coat. "It's very good," she said ingenuously. The torch's beam spilled faintly to the ground. This could be lucky, he thought. It's a place to hide until morning. "Look," he said, "How much?"

"No, no. You gentleman. You give me later. When you pleased. As you like."

He looked back towards the fires; they burned like candles worshipping the darkness.

"Come with me," she whispered. "You safe."

He pushed her hand away. She stepped back from him.

"Safe?" he said. "Why do you say that? Safe? What do you mean, I'm safe?"

"I don't mean harm," she said. "No harm."

"Do you know Durcan?"

"Durcan? What is that you say? You tell me please."

"Durcan is a man," he said. "You know him bloody well don't you?"

"A man is Durcan? No, don't know."

The torchlight shone across her legs. He wanted to believe her. It would be an escape of a sort. She took his hand and put it on her breast and whispered, "Now you see."

"You know him," Traynor said and wondered bitterly if she did or if the man had. If they weren't traps the waste was too appalling to consider. "Self-defence," he said.

"Tommy?"

He took his hand away.

"I can't take chances."

"Safe. Clean. You safe."

"No."

"Then give me something, Tommy. Something for my time. You feel it tit."

She had a new insistence. Looking at her broken teeth Traynor said "Go away" and tried to pass her. She held his arm. "Dirhams," she said. He was surprised at how much strength she had. His wife had never loved him. They had acted out the postures of commitment for a while before discovering the secret of their weakness.

"Get away," he said, trying to push her back. They could be following in silence, through the darkness. If the body had been found would the police be told at once? Or would they wait? If they were Durcan's men they might not like policemen asking questions. "Get away," he said, pulling out the empty pistol. It was not difficult to assert oneself. "You heard what I said. Get away." His hand was trembling slightly but she did not show fear. He felt humiliated by her calmness; one wanted one's assertion to be real.

His face was twitching. But I controlled it for some hours today, he thought. These small achievements were important. Strength was made from them; through them one found the disciplines.

"All right," she said. She turned and walked away. This was how it had always ended; standing there while someone walked away. If I'm being hunted should I move, he thought, or hurry or stay here? The bitter smell of charcoal came to him from where the fires were burning and a dog growled hostile warning. One avoided confrontation by delay. It seemed the wisest thing yet voices could bring panic.

He put the pistol back into his pocket. I'll see Bannister, he thought. If it were murder it was easier than one might have expected. He walked quickly towards Señora Perez's house. Two sailors staggered from an alleyway; their raucous voices acted like a screen. He thought, I'm safer now. He knew and understood these changed surroundings. It was any city late at night, the buildings were the same. There was less threat; the drunks and sounds were links with many other places. They're not following me, he thought, I just imagined voices. Nobody was there. I was attacked. He would have killed me. Like a prayer, the words brought comfort. It's a superficial wound, he thought—the joke of the patrol when they found bodies blown apart. He had not liked that painful joke. The men would sometimes sing or steal a watch. One lost respect for death, grew bored with it. And yet I don't believe that I killed anyone before. The bodies were irrelevant as mud. He knew that his face was twitching. Steady on, he thought. No need to panic. Here's the street. That light is Bannister's room. And that one's Mrs. Merton's. He tried the door but it was locked. This disconcerted him. He tried again, his fingers sweating on the handle. It was most unusual. Señora Perez, he knew, gave no one a key so had never locked it until much later. He looked at Bannister's window and said, hoarsely, "Bannister," knowing that his voice would not be heard. A plan, he thought deliberately, a plan, a plan, peering back down the street at the innocent darkness. There was no sound, no voices. He had not been followed after all. She might, he thought, have been honest. He remembered the warmth of her breast, the small hard nipple with a pang of empty regret. If I went back now. A sailor, he thought, that sailor or some other common drunk. She would forget that she had ever seen him or if she remembered it would be the

94

pistol not the face or not the touch. Perhaps she had guessed from the touch; women sometimes knew. He had seen their speculative eyes. A plan, he thought, mistakes were made through tactical short-sightedness. He went to the kitchen window. It was open at the top. He felt a sense of triumph that was very like success. He could be happy this way, finding the answers, proving himself. It was almost a little like love. A younger man would have panicked, he thought, and left traces everywhere of blood, made noise, got caught. There was no real substitute for age or for experience.

He pushed open the window and climbed awkwardly to the sill, kneeling there like a pilgrim balancing on penitential stones. He was afraid of falling. Panic was one small accident away. He felt the twitch. It's so unfair, he thought. He could not bear the chance that he might fail now. He pushed open the wooden shutters. Something moved and a can rattled in the kitchen. "Señora Perez?" he said. "Is that you there, Señora?"

Then he saw that it was just the cat. Its eyes shone brightly, up at him like a warning.

"Pussy, puss," he whispered. "Pussy, pussy," wondering if it knew him. This is absurd, he thought. He twisted and sat on the sill. His legs reached to the kitchen floor. He stood up and carefully closed the window. Everything was normal again. He was back in control. The smell of bad cooking surrounded him like a welcome. "Pussy, puss," he whispered heartily. "Where are you? That's the good little puss." The cat's eyes were no longer visible. It'll keep away from my feet, he thought, it isn't as bloody stupid as that. That door over there is to the old woman's bedroom. Over there's the one that leads to the hall. He felt his way around the wall to where he was certain he remembered the door to be. His fingers touched a cooker, brushed across a table, felt the sink, a crack, a handle.

Training, he thought, as he went out into the hall. Self-discipline. An old clock ticked noisily on a shelf. He went up the stairs, pausing for a moment outside Janet's room, listening to the voices. Was that her husband? They were speaking

95

softly. He tried unsuccessfully to hear. That's not her husband's voice is it? Maybe, he thought, it's Bannister. The idea worried him as he climbed the stairs and knocked on Bannister's door.

"Who's that?"

"Is that you, Bannister?"

"Who's there?"

"Traynor," he said. There was no reply. "Traynor," he said again. "Do you mind if I come in?"

"It's very late." Bannister's voice was doubtful. "I'll see you in the morning."

"I won't delay you. Just a couple of words. It's something rather important."

He used to be glad of visits, Traynor thought. What's all the fuss about now? It isn't that late. He turned the handle but the door had been bolted inside. The whole house has changed, he thought. They couldn't know anything, could they?

"I'll be with you in a minute," Bannister said. "If you're sure it won't keep until the morning."

"I'd prefer to see you now."

"Just a minute then."

The bed creaked like a sound of love and Bannister coughed. He opened the door. He was wearing a coat pulled over his pyjamas. He peered out nervously at Traynor.

"It *is* you," he said.

"Who did you think it was? Some girl?"

"No, no. It's just unexpected. When did you get back?"

"Not long ago. You wouldn't mind", Traynor said, "if I came in?"

"No, no. Come in of course."

The air was stale with cigarette smoke and the smell of unchanged sheets.

"I hope that I didn't wake you."

"No, you didn't," Bannister said. "I was just going to go to sleep." He buttoned up his coat and pulled a cover across the rumpled sheets of the bed. "I hadn't turned out the light."

"I noticed that. Well, Bannister, you're keeping well?" The question hung between them like an intimacy.

"Oh very well indeed. It's not my favourite time, as I think you know. It's much worse in Casablanca, I suppose?"

"It's a good deal hotter there. One is moving towards the Equator. That makes all the difference."

Traynor sat on a creaking chair and looked at a small pile of socks in an open suitcase. "I don't mind it really. Never did much, you know. Something in the blood."

"You thought that you'd be back much earlier."

Bannister could not keep a tone of accusation from his voice. "I think you said two weeks." He felt obscurely betrayed. He sat on the edge of the bed and reached for cigarettes.

"That's right," Traynor said. "That's what I thought it would be. Two weeks or three at most. But some things occurred to delay me. Unscheduled, you know." He watched as Bannister lighted a cigarette. "Was anyone making inquiries?"

"Inquiries?"

"About me?"

"What kind of inquiries?" Bannister asked. I'm on to something now, he thought. He means Abu or Farrell. Trying to get me mixed up in some plan.

"Oh nothing specific really," Traynor said. "I really only wondered. Friends. Some friends who said that they might possibly call. I wondered if I had missed them."

"I don't think", Bannister said, "that he was a friend."

"I beg your pardon? Who?"

"The visitor."

Bannister watched him closely. This, he knew, was how the game was played. "You had a visitor." Why should he sit there and give him information? Let him explain. The bastard hasn't been honest with me. "What did he want?"

"How would I know?" Bannister said. "I wasn't talking to him. Nobody was."

"Now look here, Bannister," Traynor said. It was like

coming out of a dream. He felt the fear, the need for reassurance. "What's all the bloody mystery?"

"You tell me. I think I deserve an explanation. You tell me."

"You're talking in riddles, man."

"Riddles!" Bannister said. "I hadn't thought of that. I used to like riddles. How about you? Are you good at answering them? What's the difference between a parrot and Charing Cross Station? Do you know?"

He's drunk, Traynor thought. That's all that's to it. He's absolutely drunk. But the fear did not end with the dream. It was not the effect but the cause; it went on like an ache. He thought, If that man is dead they're almost sure to find me. They'll circulate descriptions of my clothes and height and colour.

"I'd like a drink," he said. "Do you have anything by any chance?"

"No."

"Perhaps in my room. I'm not sure . . ."

"Your room isn't yours any more," Bannister said. "Didn't you know? But of course, how could you? There's a man called Farrell there, a youngish chap from Ireland. He might be the friend you were expecting."

"But it's still my room!"

"No, no, Señora Perez has let it to this other chap. I suppose she assumed that you wouldn't be coming back."

"And who is this fellow Farrell?"

"You don't know him?"

"Never heard of him. Did he tell you that he knew me?"

"No, he asked about you though. He seemed quite interested." He saw the fear spreading on Traynor's face and felt a powerful satisfaction. This was how the game was won; the steady undermining.

"When?"

"Today. He arrived here only yesterday." He stubbed out his cigarette. "If you'd been a little earlier you'd have found your room waiting. That's bad luck."

98

"It doesn't make sense," Traynor said. His face was twitching.

"It didn't make sense to me."

"You're sure that his name is Farrell?"

"That's what he said. From Ireland." Bannister reached out for his cigarettes. "I thought him rather strange," he said deliberately, watching for the reaction.

"Strange in what way?"

"Hard to describe, you know. Just strange. I wouldn't trust him. Are you wanted by the police?"

"Good God no! What made you think that?"

"I just wondered," Bannister said. "No offence. Some strange things have been happening." He could go on for ever like this, exulting in the chase, the sense of powerful play. He saw that Traynor's hands were trembling slightly.

"What kind of things have been happening?"

"I don't want to get involved."

"I really don't follow you, Bannister."

"I'm not a fool," Bannister said, feigning anger. He examined his cigarette. "There's some funny things going on. This isn't England. A man's got to watch his step."

"Did you know that I was married once?" Traynor asked unexpectedly.

Bannister was oddly shocked. He would never have guessed.

"It was something you said that reminded me. A man's got to watch his step. You did say that just now, didn't you? I didn't mishear you? She used to say something rather like that. 'I've got to watch my step.'" He wiped his eyes with the back of a trembling hand and said, "It's a long time ago."

"Is she dead?"

"I don't know. She could be, I suppose. There weren't any children." He pulled out a dirty handkerchief and patted the side of his nose.

"I didn't know," Bannister said. "You never mentioned her before."

"I don't as a rule, you see. There isn't any point. I haven't

99

even got her picture." He put the handkerchief away and looked around the room as if searching for something that he might have dropped. A spider scuttled along beside his shoes.

"It happens," Bannister said. He felt a distant envy of Traynor. Someone had loved him, however briefly and had not haggled about the price. He wanted to know more but he guessed that Traynor would not tell. There was no point in asking questions. Seances may fascinate one's dreams but there were questions that were better left unanswered. One hoped that mediums cheated, worked the lights and imitated voices, had some human way of finding out a name, a place, a date, a scene. The disembodied voices promised something so much worse than life. He said, "I nearly got married once." It was a foolish lie. Traynor was not even listening.

"Sorry. What's that?"

"It doesn't matter. Just an observation, that's all."

Somewhere in the house a board was creaking. The spider was out of sight.

"Then it looks as if I won't be able to have my room tonight."

"I doubt it," Bannister said. "But maybe, of course, if you woke Señora Perez."

"No, I won't do that. I hoped to just slip in tonight and leave quite early in the morning. Did she happen to tell the police?"

"That you were missing?"

"I thought she might have possibly complained. There's a matter of rent. A small sum. A week or two, I believe. It doesn't amount to much. But you know what she's like. They're all the same, I find. I'll send her a cheque, of course."

"I wonder," Bannister said.

The ashtray was overflowing. He cleared a space with his finger and stubbed out the cigarette. "I wonder. That visitor I mentioned. I don't know who he was. Farrell found him in your old room quite late last night, I believe. It seems that he hit Farrell and got clear away. He may have been a thief, of

100

course, but it did occur to me that he might just have thought that it was you."

"Good God," Traynor said. "You should have told me before. Was he Arab?"

"Very probably, I hear."

"I don't know who he could have been. Last night, you say? There's no mistake about that?"

Bannister saw from the rapid twitch that he must be making a guess.

"There's something odd going on. It annoys me."

"What else is odd?" Traynor asked.

"Someone's trying to involve me in something or other." Smoke came from the butt in the ashtray. He pressed it with his fingers. "I don't know who it is and I don't think I even know why."

Traynor stood up and went to the window. He tried to peer through the shutters into the darkness, his hands wedged tightly in his pockets. "I've had quite a day," he said.

"I'd better go back to bed," Bannister said impatiently.

The talk had lost its point. There was no victory here; the man was already defeated.

"What time is it?"

"I don't know. My watch has stopped. It must be fairly late."

"I have nowhere to go," Traynor said. "Can I stay here with you for even a few hours. I'm willing to pay of course. I'll be leaving early in the morning. You'd be doing me a very good turn," he added, without much hope. "I can easily sleep on the floor."

"Why should I be involved?" Bannister said. He looked uneasily at Traynor. "I don't want to be involved. Not in this. It's all too odd. I don't like it."

"But there's no question of involvement, I assure you. You know what's happened even better than I do. That damn woman's taken my room away."

"I don't know," Bannister said. "I don't want anything to do with the police. I believe that they're bloody rough when they want to, even if you're carrying a British passport. There are all sorts of old grudges left over from the international arrangement. There was a case some years ago. I forget the name." He stared at the damp spot on the ceiling. "Some fellow called Spark, I think. Yes, I think it was Spark. He was questioned for three whole days. No earthly reason for it. No justification at all. I believe that they broke his ribs...."

"Look," Traynor said, "I can't know everything that's been happening here but it had nothing to do with me. You know me better than that."

He doesn't care what happens to me, Bannister thought. He simply wants to use me. That's all. But he could not say this directly. The straight rebuff was more than he had learned. Like the shoe-shine boy, he thought with bitterness. Another small defeat.

"We've been quite good friends," Traynor said. "A good deal in common. There are very few who know that I've been married. It takes trust to tell a thing like that to someone."

The envy brought some courage.

"I'm sorry," Bannister said, "but I can't agree. I'm sure that some hotel . . ." He felt bile curdle. "That some hotel", he said, "will have an empty room." This could be a victory still. There was always a point of farther defeat to measure.

"For the sake of old times," Traynor said.

"I'm worried, Traynor. I assure you that that's the truth." A dim desire for friendship stirred in his mind. "I'm sorry." Had they really been friends? Something in common? Traynor was a much older man. The bond was in the twitch, the gins and tonics taken in the hot, unfriendly sun. "You do see my point?"

"But I wouldn't ask you, would I, if it weren't absolutely necessary to me?" He tapped his pocket. "I have money," he said.

"I'm afraid that I can't help this time," Bannister said, looking across at Traynor's visible inadequacy; the twitch, the bloodshot eyes, the hands that were beyond control. A desire for cruelty came like a new idea. He said, "Did your wife . . . ?"

102

then stopped, feeling a little afraid. One could go too far. The astuteness of failure made some farther failures avoidable.

"Anyway," Traynor said, "it's probably better not to. I've wasted enough time already. I'll go now." He went to the door and stood there like an actor who is not quite sure of his lines. He looked past Bannister; the look seemed patronizing. Bannister stirred uneasily. "All right," he said. Dislike was mixed with loneliness and fear. The spider crawled across the door; from the landing outside a board creaked.

"That might be Farrell," Bannister said. "Are you going to see him?"

"No. There's no point."

The voice was not tremulous any more; only the hands shook in the pockets.

"Very well then," Traynor said and left the room. The spider fell from the door. It lay in a ball for almost a minute then, slowly uncurling, it crawled towards Bannister.

Farrell went into his room and closed the door. It's no business of mine, he thought. The voice had sounded worried. It could have been anyone, looking for money or advice. He thought of her tears, the baby sleeping on indifferent to her needs. The voice from Bannister's room, the tears, the way she swam. He lay on the bed and closed his eyes; his face was sore and peeling from the sun. The voice had been worried; the man had sounded English; it was not enough on which to form a theory. Her innocence may be assumed, he thought. The tenderness he felt was without commitment. He remembered Catherine's innocence turning into bewilderment and then into anger. "You use me to boost yourself," she had said in the Horseshoe Bar of the Shelbourne Hotel. Beside them, two businessmen had drunk large brandies and talked about their golf. "You need to be reassured by seeing how far you can go in hurting someone. There are times when I don't even feel like a proper person."

"For God's sake!"

"Admit it, can't you."

He remembered the bracelet she was wearing and the coat and the dress and the ring that was made from a sovereign. "You like to be part of a bigger abstraction. Admit it. You like to make me unhappy!" He got up and turned on the light. The thief could come back again. There would be no warning. The memory of Catherine stayed with him like a burden.

"You don't want to know what I feel, do you? Never!"

"We'd better be going."

"You'd better, you mean. I'm not going anywhere."

The businessmen had been listening. He had wanted to protest, "Not here". Was she right or did it even matter?

He took out a notebook and sat on the edge of the bed. There were drawings on the first three pages; some faces, a cartoon-hen, a fat priest, a man climbing a ladder. He drew a girl's face; round eyes, small mouth, hair brushed back, then wrote: "I came to Tangier on the big Bland steamer, *Maroc*, from Gibraltar . . ."

# Chapter Eight

He thought about his route. The light from Bannister's window faded on the street. Down to the end, he thought, then right and right again. Five minutes' walk past tall, old houses to the row of cheap hotels. He would be much safer. No one would look for him there. It had been foolish to go to the house. They knew that he had the money. They could have found him easily but there he would be safe, anonymous. Nobody would ask questions. In a few more minutes, he thought and felt an almost buoyant sense of safety. The moon was partially hidden by a tight clenched fist of clouds. I was never a coward, never. One's nerve could be a little shaken at times. That could happen to any man. Cowardice was different; there was no cure from that disease. They did not even know what made it happen.

He went down the empty street, his fingers curled around the handle of the pistol. He should have loaded it. Fear was an accident like death or life or love. One took one's chances. A dog whined piteously in some other street. The man might not be dead. In self-defence, he thought. The shooting could be justified in law. A light went off above his head and he heard the creak of bedsprings and someone speaking. Safety, he thought, was a good night's sleep. Bannister's a bloody fool. There's no involvement. I'll go to Paris then maybe on to Rome. The mistake I made was to come back here. I should have left from some other port. That was panic. The only bad mistake. This street was ugly. All the houses seemed like remnants from an even poorer time. The dog continued whimpering, mourning for some inexplicable loss and for a moment Traynor wondered if the man in the medina might be mourned like that. It can't be helped, he thought. One took one's chances. Death was shared with strangers. Accidents could happen.

It was darker here. He walked along the narrow, sloping street. A sea-shell crunched beneath his shoe. The children played with them in the day-time, making patterns in the hot and sickly dirt. If she had loved me . . . Traynor thought. The supposition had no ending. It would be the same; love died amongst the empty patterns of deceit, the old pretences. I should have known, he whispered, walking in the darkness past a shuttered café. Cooking smells still lingered near the door. It was not her fault, he whispered. The power of the admission almost shocked him. It dispelled all the old pretences of the careful, lonely years. He gripped the pistol tightly. But if she had understood he thought, justifying himself. He turned into another street and looked for the hotels. Someone had left a chair outside a door. It worried him to see it. Why there? he wondered, peering to see if someone might be sitting there. On getting closer he saw that the chair had no seat and that one leg was badly broken. It seemed more sinister then, a mutilated remnant, like the houses. He felt the wood as if by touching it he might discover some clue that would be of interest. He stood there, knowing that it did not matter and wondering what a man should do. Perhaps he thought, my nerves. . . . Some child had played a game with it and left it there. It did not matter. It was of no significance. He was not the sort of man who lost proportions. There were better things to think about; tomorrow's flight, the happy days in Paris and perhaps, in Rome. He walked on a little farther, trying to hum a tune that he had known once. He could not get it right. Some part of the melody had gone. I'm rich, he thought, and free.

He saw the dim hotel lights.

# PART TWO

# Chapter One

"I know what you mean," the Inspector said. "Sad. Very sad. Excuse me." He turned away to yawn and Bannister shifted furtively on the bed. He felt outraged and frightened. Threatening heat came through his open window like another phrase or question that he could not understand. The Inspector looked at him again with acquiescent eyes. "A climate such as this", he said, "is only for the natives." He looked at a piece of paper. "Mr. Bannister," he read. "I know exactly what you mean." He walked across to the window and looked down at the noisy street. "Your view", he said, "is all right. I like a view. The sea, perhaps, or hills. You sleep long, Mr. Bannister?"

"Sleep long?"

"For many hours? You sleep soundly?"

"Oh quite well," Bannister said. The senseless questions were like disembodied voices in a darkened room, his hand gripped tightly, fear and hope around him. "Why do you ask?" he said.

"My curiosity." The Inspector smiled and Bannister stirred uneasily. "Myself I sleep long. Not last night. Last night no sleep at all." He stroked his chin. "I like the air," he said. His short, plump fingers seemed to be stroking a beard that was not there.

"Really?" Bannister said. He swallowed dryness. It was like making small talk in a train; the words, to begin with, were never entirely innocent of menace. One went on facing the humiliations that could not be avoided.

"Yes," the Inspector said. "This night, did you sleep long or short, Mr. Bannister?"

"I slept quite well."

"From early?"

The eyes remained acquiescent but the voice seemed doubtful.

"Perhaps if you explained", Bannister said, "the point of the visit. I don't understand the questions or what you're doing here. If I knew what you were looking for, perhaps . . ."

"I'm not looking for anything."

"Isn't it rather unusual then? That you're here in my room? So early in the morning. I really don't understand." He sat with his hands on his knees like an elderly peasant. The sun was making him blink.

"It's simple," the Inspector said. He walked around the room, looking more proprietorial than Bannister had ever felt. "Some things occur this night." He stood beside the door and smiled. "These things they keep me from sleep. I must now find out why they happen. You might think that you should help."

"I doubt if I can."

"You can not be sure, Mr. Bannister." He seemed to have learned the name. He did not read it from his notes. He put them away and his smile went on like mockery.

"Perhaps you can help me very much."

"What happened?"

"No, you must tell me, Mr. Bannister, what happened. You understand? That's how we start."

He leaned against the door and held up one foot to inspect a dusty shoe.

"You need not hurry," he said pleasantly. "I will not try to make you go so fast." The creak and clatter of carts went on unbroken from the street. It might have been the sound of refugees.

"Well," Bannister said. He tried to calm himself but felt an active hatred for the young, fat face that stared at him with interest. "Nothing happened."

"Nothing at all?"

"Just more or less the same as any other night." I'll deny that Traynor was here, he thought. They could never prove it. No one could have seen him last night. I didn't ask him to come. The smile was like poison; behind the deceptive front the menace lurked. He said, "It's sometimes difficult to remember everything." The Inspector nodded his head, "That is true. You must try." The voice seemed sympathetic. One could even believe that he cared or understood.

"I slept quite well," Bannister said, and thought obscurely of Traynor's wife. "I usually do."

"And before you sleep?"

The change in the Inspector's voice was almost imperceptible but Bannister recognised it.

"Before that," he said. "I had a drink or two and a meal. Then I came home here and went to bed." He was ashamed of the uneventfulness of the evening; it marked him out as a failure. "I'm not in good health," he explained. "I have to take things easy."

"That is sad," the Inspector said. He took a step forward. "Will you now tell me please who it was that you were talking to?"

"I wasn't talking to anyone."

"No person? You must have said words to some person!"

"I met no one. Earlier in the day I met Farrell. He's a chap with a room upstairs. I had a drink with him."

"Mr. Farrell and you. You are friends?"

"I met him yesterday for the first time."

"I see." The Inspector frowned. His clothes needed to be brushed. "You say you talk to no one else?"

"No," Bannister said. He felt a kind of defiance. There was something vaguely wrong. "My solicitor should be here," he said, then wondered if the laws were even the same. There was so much than one did not know. "I could accidentally incriminate myself."

"That is not possible, Mr. Bannister. This is a talk. We talk. You, me. Like this," he said confidentially, "the persons in this house. You tell me about them, yes?"

"I'm not much of a mixer," Bannister said. "My health . . ." The excuse appealed to him. He coughed and lost some of the shame.

"The woman Perez. She does not interest me a big deal."
The Inspector seemed to savour the phrases. "The woman
Perez," he said again, "a big deal. Other two. Tell me please
what you think."

"I have impressions," Bannister said slowly, trying to sound
confident again. "I'm not a man to jump to conclusions, you
understand. I don't meddle where I'm not wanted." The
Inspector smiled. It was impossible to know if he were impressed. The smile gave nothing away. That fellow Spark,
Bannister thought, his ribs were broken. All of them, someone
told me. It had happened during the questioning. People
were vague about the details. Spark had done nothing at all.
He looked down at the Inspector's dusty shoes and said. "I
can hardly say anything about Farrell. He arrived just the day
before yesterday. I believe that he comes from Ireland."

"I believe so," the Inspector said. He smiled quite cheerfully. "The other lady?"

"Mrs. Merton? Oh, she's been here for a couple of months.
Her husband is somewhat odd." He hoped that all this would
hide the habitual actions of his evening and the unexpected
visit. "He's some kind of writer, I believe, Señora Perez said.
Or something like that. He's hardly ever here."

"But his wife, she must be lonely then?"

The question seemed casual. "I don't know," Bannister
said. "She's rather a nice girl, I think."

The Inspector smiled.

"Perhaps she has a friend," he said. "A friend who can
love her more than her husband can. You might, Mr. Bannister, know about that thing? A friend who is not always
away?"

The insinuation interested Bannister. He took out cigarettes.
The Inspector shook his head. "No thank you." Bannister
lighted one for himself and said, "Well these things happen
of course." The false trail promised an easy escape. "As a
matter of fact," he said vindictively, "I think I heard someone
in her room last night."

"It was a man you hear?"

"Well I just heard the voice. It was certainly a man's. . . ."

"Do you know what man?"

"No."

"Think, Mr. Bannister, think. Was it Mr. Traynor's voice? Señora Perez she tell me you were good friend to Mr. Traynor. Could it be Mr. Traynor?"

Bannister tasted fear. It seeped slowly and bitterly into the dryness of his mouth. There were escapes and new imprisonments on every trail. The laws were made by others.

"Traynor?" he said, pausing, trying to seem surprised. "He hasn't been here for ages. It certainly wasn't Traynor."

"Was it not?" the Inspector said. He laughed gently. "I did not think so, no. Mr. Traynor was not good man for the girls. Was it this Mr. Farrell?" He closed his eyes. "Or some other person?" The eyelids were strangely pale. They seemed like cartoon-eyes, drawn clumsily on the fat, impassive face. Bannister stared at them in horror as if he were being forced to see some cruelly freakish trick.

"It might have been," he said. It seemed quite pointless to be talking to someone who could not see.

"I was afraid, Mr. Bannister," the Inspector said, "that you might not want to give me help." He opened his eyes but stared past Bannister's shoulder at the wall. "Now you help me. That is good. So Farrell was in her room?"

"I said that it might have been him. I can't possibly be certain. I merely heard a voice."

"It is right that you are cautious. That seems good. This is a cautious country, Mr. Bannister. To go against that is not wise. Trouble. Yet caution can cause trouble as well. As with love, Mr. Bannister." The monotonous voice went on like a meaningless incantation; it might have been summoned in darkness.

He must guess that Traynor was here, Bannister thought, looking away from the impassively smiling face. The Inspector had loosened his tie.

"Mr. Traynor died last night."

"Dead? He couldn't be dead."

"Why could he not?"

"But he isn't an old man. His health was good."

"No other reason, Mr. Bannister?"

"The surprise. . . ."

"It kept me from my bed. No long sleep. I wonder, Mr. Bannister," the voice seemed filled with humour and affection, "if you knew that."

"How could I possibly know it? I haven't seen him for weeks. The last time I saw him he seemed perfectly healthy to me. Old soldiers, you know," Bannister said, staring at the Inspector's face as if he had been accused of murder.

"He was killed," the Inspector said. "Near to here. Some person stabbed him many times. Stabbings in the neck. That person must have had a reason." He smiled and shook his head. "You were his friend. Tell me please who did not like him."

"No, we weren't friends. I want to make that absolutely clear." For a moment he regretted the small betrayal of Britain and the gins and tonics in the sun, the short, dull conversations. "I knew nothing about his business."

"Where did Mr. Traynor go?"

"To Casablanca."

"He told you that he was going there?"

"He just mentioned it," Bannister said. "In passing. It was merely a casual remark." He must have known last night when he came here, he thought, remembering Traynor's face. He stood up, swallowing the taste in his mouth. "I'm naturally shocked," he said and thought, If I say anything at all I'll be involved. Abu knows something. Maybe Farrell does as well. They could all be involved without my knowing it. I can't afford any scandal.

"You are shocked of course. When a loved friend dies, Mr. Bannister. . . ."

"I told you that he wasn't a friend."

"You knew him well. The shock would be great. I am accustomed . . . yes? . . . to death. I see much of it. It is a part of my day. But even to myself if a close friend of my own . . ."

"Now look here," Bannister said. "You keep on suggesting that I was a friend. I've told you several times already . . ."

"You will mourn, Mr. Bannister?"

"I'm sorry, of course, that he's dead. I sometimes enjoyed his company. Being British," he said. He looked across hopefully at the Inspector. "We had something in common that way."

"I understand, Mr. Bannister. I come here to tell you the news. I will come back again to see if you remember anything that may be useful for me. Meeting with you was very happy for me."

Bannister watched him walking down the street. The children did not go near him. An old man bowed; the gesture, like a self-destructive act, seemed made from fear and pride. It wasn't any good pretending, Bannister thought, that this would all pass over. This was how fate moved; it hemmed one in with accidents and irony like this. The irony of Traynor's death was like the accident of his birth; he had no choice to make. Stabbed in the neck. They're bloody savage, he thought, with indignation. The Inspector's smile might have been imprinted on the room.

He moved away from the window; the floorboards creaked; this was the size of the world. The voices had promised nothing but supervision; the dead eyes watched from the walls. She shouldn't have told him we were friends, he thought, resentfully. He went downstairs. Señora Perez was standing in the hall.

"Now look at the trouble," she said.

He looked around as if the body might be there. The cat came up the passage, its tail erect, dislike gleaming from its eyes.

"The trouble and shame," she said. "Police inside my house."

He saw that she had been crying but felt no pity for her. The tears were smudged across her ugly face. "Jamás me olvido de una cara!" she said. "I have seen that man before.

That police. But where?" She looked at Bannister with moist, accusing eyes. She seemed to be older but behind the tears, he knew that anger waited like an assassin.

"I suppose that he told you about Traynor."

"Told me. Yes he told me. Yes. Told me. Dead with a knife. Did you love with him he asked me. To mock me." The cat's eyes stared at Bannister like a hypnotist's device. "To mock me. To say that I do bad things. Yes. He said that."

She emphasized her words as if she had been contradicted. "I know from the way that he looked at me and laughed. He is an evil man. Pagan. All of them. No good."

"I'm sure that he meant no harm," Bannister said. He was suddenly anxious to placate her. One needed someone, anyone, on one's side.

"They're inefficient," he said. "And corrupt, of course." The thought of Traynor's death was already becoming less real. "Perhaps if we just forget."

"No forget," she shouted. "Ladnos!"

He moved away from her, startled. She followed him. He stopped, feeling ridiculous and saw the cat go stalking up the stairs. "I beg your pardon," he said. "I thought . . ."

"No forget," she shouted again. "Insult. To me. Too many troubles now."

"It has been trying, I must agree."

"Insult. Police and things in my house. In this my house." She pointed, trembling, at the wall.

"I think I'll take my stroll," he said. "Perhaps some other time we can talk."

"Someone in my house is evil. Why should I allow that, please?"

"Perhaps Mr. Farrell," he said, noticing that her fists were clenched.

"He not here. That policeman he asked where he was. He went out early, I told him. How would I know? And so did that Mrs. Merton. She takes her baby."

"Did they go out together?"

Bannister found that he was interested again and less unsure. Perhaps she could be an ally.

"No, that Mr. Farrell went out first. Then Mrs. Merton.
Mr. Bannister," she said and he guessed that tears were not far
away, "it should not happen. Not in this my house."

"I quite agree with you," he said. "It's most unsettling."
Her indignation offered him hope. He thought, I'll take the
plunge, and said, "If I can be of any help please don't hesitate
to ask." He felt a kind of friendship reaching out between
them, a token of affinity. "In any way." This was, perhaps,
the way that one learned to love, this hope and satisfaction.

"How do I know who to trust?" she said.

"I can assure you," he groped around for the words, "my
dear Señora Perez, that I'm worthy of your fullest trust."

She went into the kitchen. "I don't know that," she said,
closing the door behind her. The hallway became much
darker. They're all the same, he thought with some bewilderment as he went out to the dusty street.

# Chapter Two

Janet felt uncomfortable on the beach. It might have been a stretch of desert. In the distance the flat band of sea glistened like a mirage. Only the railway line behind her back could threaten the illusion. One paid a price for peace; the safety of others and of oneself. He's perfectly safe, she thought, looking up at the sky through half-closed eyes. The blue monotony could get on one's nerves. She picked up hot, dry sand and let it run out, slowly, between her fingers. Gulls flapped listlessly across the band of sea.

We *have* been happy, she thought. Her fingers tasted of salt. If he were back again, the three of us. . . . She turned her head away as if he were there explaining, assuming she would understand. If I could only cry. In love one moved towards moderation like a vice. One gave a little less away each time, pretending that it made no difference. The only fear was that one might not be entirely self-sufficient. Something was lost. She could understand the Muslims' fear of portraits, cameras; leaving a shadow of oneself behind in someone else's mind. The shared uneasiness, the earnest talk, the single iron bed; the protestations of fulfilment and the tears.

He trusts me now, she thought, wherever he is I know that he trusts me now. Trust, like an anchor, held her closely to his ill-conceived ideas. I wonder if it even occurred to him to worry about it, she thought. "I'm going home," she said, looking around in case someone had heard but there was no one there. Her footprints marked a way across the sand. The café wall was glinting whitely in the distance.

She closed her eyes. There was not much time left. The crowd would soon be down to start its day. Or maybe the boys would come to stare at her again, their lusts like little accusations in the heat. A train would soon pass by, she knew, the engine belching steam. She stroked the hot, dry sand and thought with disappointment, No, I'm not going home. I'll stay here, waiting, trusted. Choices were deceptive things. They were so often made before one even suspected. "Johnny's all right," she said but this time did not bother to look around. There could not be anyone there. The shrieks of the gulls were growing like a protest. It was an evening sound. Why do they shriek? she wondered without much interest, feeling sweat gather across her face. It might be love, suspicion, anything but trust. If I weren't married. . . . The thought of Johnny drove the rest of the feeling away. She felt pity for him, waiting innocent and unknowing in the café, showing the hopelessness and helplessness and awful power of trust.

"You're here early," Farrell said.

She sat up, startled and heard the train come beating along the line. He was standing close to her.

"You frightened me," she said.

"I'm very sorry. Did you not see me coming? I waved." He sat down beside her and took out cigarettes. Two matches would not light. "They must be damp," he said. The third one flared.

"I think I was half-asleep."

"You'd want to watch the sun. Where's Johnny?"

"In the café."

"They must open very early."

"She's really very decent," Janet said. "She has a little boy of her own. I bring him presents. He's the most beautiful child." The train rattled past, the driver laughing and flexing his arm.

Farrell said, "I wondered if the pedlar might be here this morning. Do you think so?"

"He might," she said with disappointment. Perhaps one was marked by trust. Did it stare like some disturbance from one's eyes? She looked after the train, the open carriages rocking, the goods piled high under dirty green canvas. The steam came up like a code that no one could read and faded against the sky.

"You didn't have a swim yet?"

"No. I didn't like to", she said, "with nobody here. And the tide is so far out."

"I hope that I didn't upset you too much last night."

She felt a slight resentment; the assumption that she had cared was too easily made.

"Oh no," she said. "It was nice."

He touched her arm; she looked away from him.

"Janet," he said, gripping her arm tightly. She turned to him and smiled. "I don't give a damn about pedlars."

"Oh you do," she said. "You care about them all right."

"Only sometimes. I know you think it's foolish."

His fingers were hurting her. I'm trusted, she thought, but it mustn't show through now. She loosened his fingers. "I don't suppose", she said, "that you'd like a swim."

"Why not?"

"It may be cold."

"All the better." He took off his shirt. "I'm willing to chance it," he said. "It looks good anyway."

I have to learn the whole thing over again, she thought, the tone of voice, the half-meant words, the words that mean more than they say. The language was never the same. She thought for a moment of Johnny and felt a little sadness. But he'll still be loved, I love him. A gull screamed past their heads like sudden enemy fire. The sea seemed impossibly far away.

"All right," she said. "We will." She unbuttoned her blouse. Like Farrell, she was wearing a swimming-suit beneath her other clothes. All that mattered now was some kind of happiness. One could grow old quickly, alone and constantly afraid. It didn't really matter if he liked her or not. It would still be a kind of freedom. He laughed when she folded her jeans. "Convent neatness," he said. "Only Irish girls do that."

"Do what?" she asked, annoyed.

"Get cross when someone laughs at them," he said. "Come on now. "Hurry."

"I like to be tidy," she said, still feeling annoyed and conventional and disappointing.

"You can teach me to swim," he said.

They walked down to the sea. I don't want a possessive love, she thought. But casual expectations of loyalty could bind one more tightly than suspicion. She could not help comparing him with David. He said, "Watch that piece of glass," reaching out and taking her hand. She was prepared for him to say something about carelessness.

He said, "I wouldn't like you to get cut." One had to learn a new set of predictions.

The water was cold. It moved around their feet. "You go out first," he said and splashed her. She waded out and floated on her back and felt a relaxation that was almost unfamiliar. It could be a lovely day. It did not matter whether or not he loved her. She would be free. She did not care if it were meaningless to him. He would never know the role that he was playing. She watched him swim slowly towards some rocks as a motor boat came droning from the harbour, gulls gathering in its wake.

I'm living in the present now, she thought, I'm not depending on the future. He reached the rocks and waved to her. She swam a little; water-weeds like feathers curled beneath her and the sunlight was reflected by small, blood-red stones.

"I can't swim that far."

"Of course you can."

"I can't."

"I'm coming back."

She reached the beach and waited.

"That was nice," she said.

"You didn't overtax yourself."

"We can't all be so active."

This was how she spoke to David; disappointments barely hidden by a deprecating humour. He would have failed to recognize the tone.

121

"You're cross about something," Farrell said.

"You told me yesterday that I swam well."

"But you do."

"Not very. Still . . ."

It's going wrong, she thought, it doesn't matter what he thinks. Why should I care? she laughed and watched the motor boat scrawl foam across the water.

"You're like me," he said.

She looked at him quickly, puzzled.

"You like a little praise."

"Doesn't everyone?"

"Not everyone."

"Everyone that I know does."

"Then you're lucky," he said. "People are so much easier to understand when they do."

"Now the day is starting," she said. Some girls had come in a noisy group to the beach. Their towels and shouts, an open umbrella, made illusion impossible. "It was like a desert earlier", she said, "when I came down first. Sometimes I hate people, do you?"

"Nearly all of the time."

"Oh come on now," she said. "You can't just generalize. It's pretentious. I forgot to ask how your head was?"

"Much better."

They walked back towards their clothes. He did not take her hand. "To tell you the truth," he said, "there's no pain at all."

"That's good."

She felt secure. She could easily learn not to care about what he thought. It could be an arrangement, uncomplicated by doubt or love or obligation. Her obligation waited in a café, demanding love as if in revenge or payment. She said, "I'll have to go soon." He took her hand.

"Not yet."

"To look after Johnny."

"Not yet."

"He has to be fed, you know."

"He looked very fat to me. You should put him on a diet."

Sand stuck to their bodies then fell away as the sun dried the dampness. A cloud had appeared in the sky. It was almost transparent.

"It looks like a cobweb," she said. "Or those things after frost, on the hedges."

"Do you like the brooch?" he asked.

"The brooch? Oh yes. I meant to wear it today. But I wish you'd let me pay you for it. You're thinking about the pedlar aren't you?"

"I'm thinking about you."

"I doubt it," she said with involuntary diffidence.

"I thought that you liked to be praised?"

"That isn't necessarily praise."

"Then you obviously don't know what I'm thinking about you." She picked up her towel and rubbed at her hair. It may be condescension, she thought. He had a way of changing the conversation that made her especially vigilant.

"I wonder", she said, "if I really do like to be praised. On second thoughts I think that it irritates me. I seldom believe it anyway." The towel covered her face.

"You're just like a Muslim's wife," he said. "His third or fourth. I think that the fashion suits you."

She took the towel away and saw that he was smiling.

"Why did you ask me to stay?"

"Because I didn't want you to go."

It sounded too simple. She knew that she should not believe him.

"To put down the time?" she asked.

"To try to talk to you."

"Is it all that difficult?"

"It isn't all that easy," he said.

"That's very flattering."

He took her hand again with what seemed like hesitation. "Did I tell you about the man", he asked, "that I saw in Gibraltar? A madman, shouting in the street?"

"I don't think so."

"I can't understand", he said, "why he impressed me so much but he did. I think of him often."

He stroked her arm. A whore must feel this way, she thought. It was mutual detachment. He was looking away; his fingers moved along her arm like a small escape from boredom. "It struck me at the time", he said, "that he was, perhaps, the most honest man in the place. He meant what he said. Completely. You don't have to tell me that the thought is trite. But I couldn't help thinking when I saw him and listened to him how seldom we really say what we mean. Or feel what we should feel, perhaps. Or even know. We act out a complex convention. Children are different. If one could retain one's childhood's honesty one would certainly be mad."

She lay back on the sand, the towel beneath her head and heard the girls shrieking in the water. The heat was growing more intense; a faint smell of decay came from somewhere near by. Detachments lasted for minutes; indifference was even more difficult to preserve than love. We could move towards trust, she thought, while betraying David and that would be just too much to tolerate. The same traps were set, baited and waiting as one went towards every new feeling.

"I'm an honest person," she said and waited to be contradicted.

"Perhaps you are."

"You aren't?"

"Only sometimes," he said.

"Do you try to be?"

"Sometimes. It isn't always worth it."

"Why not?" she asked without much interest and a fly buzzed angrily against her arm. She brushed it away and thought of David. She had seen him fool himself too often to be fooled. She had seen him put on sincerity like a false moustache.

"Different reasons," Farrell said. "It's usually something to do with pride or esteem or love."

He lay beside her.

"Where will you go from here?"

"To Paris, I think," she said.

"That's nice."

"I've never been there before."

"You'll like it," he said. "It's about a hundred and fifty times nicer than Tangier. As long as you keep away from the gendarmerie. You should get a room near the Halles. They're going to knock them down and build God knows what. Or St. Denis. Or near the Place de la République. I'd be happy living there. I hope to some day."

"I'd better go," she said.

He turned and kissed her gently.

"Are *you* being honest?" she asked when he moved away.

"In my way. Are you?"

"I'm married."

"I don't think that that's an answer."

She knew that he had felt the fear and doubt in her kiss. There were several ways of lying. "I want to be happy," she said. "My husband trusts me."

"Are those statements incompatible?" he asked.

I'm blurting it out, she thought. The girls' screams came like ecstasy from the sea and she remembered all her grievances. Well this, she thought, is the way that one wipes them out, the big and trivial way. "I love my baby," she said, defining herself through all his insistent hungers, "You needn't believe that if you don't want to. It doesn't matter to me what you think."

"I believe you do," he said.

"But you don't see why I should?"

"I didn't say that."

"You implied it last night," she said, rebuking herself for having failed again at not caring. "I'll admit that I'm confused."

"Please don't be," he said.

"If I cry now I'll get so bloody angry."

"Do you feel like crying?"

"No," she said, and thought, Perhaps I amn't a failure at all. I could humiliate him now.

"Those girls", he said, "are getting on my nerves."

"And the smell. Do *you* smell something?"

"It must be a fish", he said, "washed up by the tide."

"I really hate it here. What you said about Paris. . . ."

"I like it here," he said. "Oh Paris is nicer, of course. But it's more respectable. Life is a little more planned."

"Do you like Dublin?"

"In the way that I like my face in the mirror in the morning," he said. "It's something you're stuck with. I like some things about it. Neary's and Herbert Park."

"Grafton Street on Saturday morning?"

"Not much," he said. "Bewley's buns."

"And people you know."

"That's why I don't care for it much."

"You seem to like a touch of mystery," she said. "The solitary figure going along like a shadow and things that go bump in the night. Isn't that adolescence?" He laughed and she watched him, wondering why she had wanted, for even a moment, to hurt him. The smell of corruption lay around them like some old, half-remembered dispute. Another train was passing but they did not turn.

"Do you know La Rochefoucauld?" he asked. " 'The effort we make to remain faithful to someone we love is little better than infidelity.' "

"That's cynical."

"Do you think so?"

"And smug."

"Surely not smug?"

"On your part," she said, "not on his. If you think it's appropriate to anything we've talked about, you're certainly very smug."

"I suppose that's possible," he said. "How do *you* deal with smugness?"

She looked away towards the sea.

"I wish that you hadn't asked me to stay here. I've just delayed. And Johnny . . ."

"You'll stay faithful to him?"

"I should have gone. There's no point . . ."

"Please Janet," he said.

His hand was on her breast; tightening. She could have cried with relief and with shame.

"Not here," she said.

"No. But somewhere."

She stood up.

"You're beautiful."

"Thank you."

She picked up her clothes. He was watching her, smugly perhaps, but the shame did not last. It was all much too easy for that. A beach-ball bounced past and children shouted with excitement.

"You might as well stay here," she said. "I'm bringing Johnny back to the house."

"I'd like to walk with you."

"No. I'd prefer if you didn't."

"And later? May I see you then?"

"If you want to."

"I want to."

"But don't be too smug," she said. "I've had enough of that."

She walked to the café, seeing the trail of her footprints going back to where he was sitting. It can mean what I want it to mean. It's a casual thing. I'm not owned. And I didn't ask to be trusted. If he didn't go away or lie . . .

A man came towards her, shuffling along on the sand.

"Lovely morning," he said as they passed. "Lots of sun. Hope it lasts."

There was something familiar about him; the suit, the tie and the voice. She remembered then; she had seen him embracing the boy. At the start it had shocked her, those open embraces on the sand and the small girls eagerly watching and giggling in a natural failure of understanding. But one got used to it as one could get used to almost anything, she thought. It was cool in the café. Light filtered through the shutters to the blue-tiled floor and the white tops of the little tables and the low white counter.

"Johnny sleep," the woman said and smiled at Janet, brushing thin hair back from her forehead. "Sleep."

"Thank you very much."

"No thank. A good boy."

"I hope that he wasn't too much trouble."

"No, he sleep."

The baby lay behind the counter in a padded wooden crib. When Janet picked him up he woke but did not cry.

"Good boy," the woman said. "He will be tall."

"And how is Salim today?"

"No, not good today." The woman wiped the counter with a cloth. "Some sick," she said.

"I'm very sorry," Janet said. "You should have told me earlier." She held Johnny tightly, wondering if the sickness might have spread. "Is he . . . ?"

"Just short time ago. My mother tends him." She pointed at a door behind the counter. Janet saw that she had been crying. There was a darkness beneath her large, brown, hungry eyes.

"If I can help."

"No, no." She shook her head. "Mother."

"Is it a fever?"

"Fever?"

"Temperature?" She put her hand on Johnny's forehead.

"Yes." The woman nodded. "Hot." She stared at Janet anxiously.

"Would you like me to see him. I might know something."

"No. My mother tends him now."

"You'll get a doctor, won't you?"

"Yes. A doctor, I think. It may not be too sick. Small boys they get these things." She smiled without conviction.

Janet said, "I'm sure that it isn't anything really," and

wondered guiltily if her worry showed. Johnny seemed perfectly well. "Are you sure that there's nothing I can do?"

"No, no. You tend your Johnny."

"You will let me know though, won't you?"

"Thank you."

"I'd say that it's probably only a chill."

The woman smiled without comprehension and said, "You
come again?"

"Of course. I'll call to see how Salim is."

"Good."

Oh God, please don't let Johnny be sick, she thought. The
baby smiled contentedly in her arms. She bent and kissed his
forehead. He fingered her cheek and smiled. She held him
tightly, walking along the beach, the towel beneath her arm.
Salim always looked healthy, she thought, he shone like silver.
"I never left you there long," she whispered. "If I had only
known . . ." The baby hiccupped loudly, looked startled and
started to cry.

# Chapter Three

Bannister looked nervously at the other men in the café. They may be police, he thought, but nobody seemed to be paying him any attention. He sat near the wall at the back of the spacious room. He had not taken off his coat; his hat was on the table. An old waiter stood in the doorway and watched the tourists going past. He had limped across to Bannister with a cup of coffee, his face tight with concentration as if he were trying to remember a name or a number. He's peculiar, Bannister thought, and drank the bitter coffee as slowly as possible. Another day to be put down.

If one knew the language; if one could only eavesdrop. They may be talking about the murder. He had bought a phrase-book once and had stared at it a few times before putting it on top of the wardrobe. He wished that he had persisted; the years were full of plans like phrase-books put aside. They crumbled away with time; heat brought a slow, persistent kind of decay. And forty-six is much too old to learn new tricks, he thought. He scratched his cheek and stared morosely at the waiter. Poor Traynor, he thought, I wonder where the funeral . . . ? Is one supposed to send a wreath? But there would be nobody there to expect it. Nobody would know or care. His wife should be informed. Poor Traynor, dead with no one there to mourn him. I won't go, he thought. These things depress me. "Another coffee," he called, pointing to his cup as the waiter turned away from the doorway and stared. "Coffee." No idea of manners of course, no sense of occasion. The old-world courtesies appealed to him; the deferential nod and being addressed as "sir". The shabby overcoat took him away from all that. One left a decent world when things began to crumble. Even if the coat were good there was something that people began to recognize.

What had Traynor found? To die like that must mean that one had lived outside the normal world. The twitch, the gins and tonics; these were merely spies sent back in an attempt to keep in contact. Foolish, Bannister thought, and felt a kind of foolish envy stirring like remorse. The death was awful but the life must have had some kind of excitement. Espionage, he thought, the world of paperback books that he had read; the fights so easily won, the drink, the travel, nights of easy sex.

The taste of coffee stayed like sickness, hard and gritty, on his tongue. I'm too often alone, he thought, and one can lose perspective. Friendship must be easy. If one could discover the rules; the game was played by every kind of man.

Two men at a near by table were arguing loudly. One of them was very old. His skin had crumbled away like paper in the sun but his voice was loud and determined. You'd think they'd do their fighting somewhere else. In private, Bannister thought, and listened as the talk went on, the strange emotions, meaningless as the words.

"One coff?"

"Yes." He saw that some had spilled into the heavy blue saucer. "Excuse me." The waiter paused from walking away and said, "Some other thing?"

"No thank you," Bannister said. "This café. Is it old?"

"Here? Old? Yes, old. Two years maybe. Maybe three."

"Oh, not too old then."

"No."

"A funny thing," Bannister said. "It seems much older. The walls . . ."

The waiter shrugged.

"Maybe three, maybe four."

"You haven't been here too long, then?"

"No, not long."

"Not longer than four years anyway," Bannister said, hoping that the man would laugh. One made acquaintances through humour; this was the way that friendship worked. The waiter shrugged again.

"Tell me," Bannister said. He lowered his voice to what he hoped would seem like a confidential tone. "I hear that some Englishman was killed last night. I believe that he was murdered. Is it in the newspaper?"

"No."

"You've read the paper?"

"No," the waiter said.

"Really? Perhaps you'd take a look and see. I heard a rumour somewhere. Rumour," he repeated loudly as the waiter remained impassive. His face was dark and lined. If one could read these hieroglyphics one could learn to say the right thing, find a pattern of pain, regret or pleasure that would respond. "I'd like to know the details. Just a matter of interest, you understand?"

The waiter smiled and this was somehow more disconcerting than the blankness. It seemed to Bannister that an ardent avarice was revealed by the brighter eyes, the broken teeth. It was here that the rules were needed.

"The man who died. He was a friend?"

"No. I don't even know who he was. Someone mentioned it to me. I believe that he might have been British. I'm British," he added as if this would make a difference.

"You want the information?"

"Not information. No." The word had too many complex implications. One paid for information. It was not exchanged in an atmosphere of ease. "Just whatever it says in the papers. Some details. I don't understand the language, you see."

"There is nothing in the paper."

"But how could you know that", Bannister said, "if you haven't even read it?" It occurred to him then that the man had much better English than one might have expected. He looked away, worried, and saw that the men who had argued were silently watching. They might be police. The whole bloody place could be full of police and he just wouldn't know. He shouldn't have opened his mouth.

"Don't worry," he said.

"Excuse me?"

"Don't worry, I said. It doesn't matter in the least. I just thought that you might have heard something." He paid for the coffee and added a small coin as a tip. The waiter did not thank him. He shrugged his shoulders and limped away to the door where he stood again like a sentry. If this were England, Bannister thought, seeming to remember comforts and civilities that he had never experienced there. One could read one's paper over a cup of coffee, have a friendly word with the waiter. It was surely a more ordered world than this one of accident piled on incomprehension. An old-fashioned telephone fixed to the wall on a bracket rang hoarsely. The waiter answered. They haven't got telephones usually, Bannister thought and watched the waiter's back as if at any moment he would turn and point. The two men were arguing again but their voices were muted now. The older man was less emphatic in his speech. The other was gesticulating like a man on a box at a racecourse. The waiter put the 'phone back on the bracket and stood there scratching the side of his neck. This could be the world of Traynor, Bannister thought, the secret signs, the message that was meant for someone else. It was not worth the strain. The funeral, he thought again. Perhaps there'll be someone there who knew . . . but he would keep away. He would not get involved. A few gins and tonics, some ten-minute conversations had not put him in Traynor's debt. There were too many risks as things were, the sun and the problems with money. The coffee was only lukewarm. He drank some and winced. It would soon be time for a proper drink, the first one of the day. It relaxed him. His nerves were naturally on edge. The talk with Traynor had upset him last night and then that Inspector this morning, the questions probing for nerve after jumping nerve. One would at least be prepared the next time; one could have a story, a manner, a sense of confidence. One would not be caught like a fool, not knowing what to say.

The waiter had gone through the curtains. The two men left the café and stood on the dusty pavement outside. Some people had so much to talk about, endlessly giving opinions,

133

asserting their minds. It was easier for some, apparently, Bannister thought, but it had not been easy for Traynor. He had never had much to talk about; the weather, comments on the heat and the foibles of Señora Perez, an occasional memory of war. If I had been in the war ... there was, at least, a kind of *camaraderie*, a club that one could join. But poor old Traynor hadn't got that much out of it.

He left the café before the waiter came back and walked along the street. Just nerves, he thought, policemen don't sit around like that. Just nerves. The heat is bloody awful. Children swarmed around him, looking for coins. "Go away," he said without conviction, remembering the shoe-shine boy. "Go away, I said." A small girl made a vulgar gesture and the others laughed too loudly; the rot began in childhood. He walked on, bitterly ashamed at being so ineffectual. They'd get tired of following, tired of mocking; they would eventually find somebody else. He passed a fountain; the thin jets of water formed reluctant, sagging arches. The shops here were European. He paused at a travel agent's and looked at the colourful posters. A beach in the south of France, tall girls with lithe, brown bodies, but the sun looked relentless. A mountain in Finland, snow and people preparing to ski ... another thing that he could not do. If I could drive a car, go down the coast. ... A yeoman standing before the Tower of London. He seemed to remember that or maybe he had seen it in some book or magazine. If I wrote to Stella again, explained ... his sister would be forty-nine years old. If I wrote, he thought with bitterness, she wouldn't even reply. Or she'd just be the same as before. She's under that bloody man's thumb, does everything he tells her to. Water is thicker than blood. He found a table outside Abu's café. He might hear something about Traynor. Abu must know. If I had been involved, he thought, the same would have happened to me. He knew that he would dream about this in different ways, each terrifyingly real.

"I'm so glad to see you, Mr. Bannister."

The gold teeth glinted like happiness in the sun.

"It has been a few days, I think. Have you not been served?" Abu beckoned for a waiter. "A gin and tonic?"

"Will you join me for something?"

"No, but it's very good of you to ask. I've had some tea. Most refreshing. How have you been keeping?"

Bannister took off his hat.

"Oh very well," he said, wiping sweat from the top of his head. "I believe that I owe you some money. Your account, if you have it. . . ." He took out some notes.

"No, no, you don't. No, no." Abu smiled an almost friendly smile. "I clearly remember asking you to be my guest." He sat down.

"You've heard about Traynor?" Bannister asked.

"What a dreadful thing," Abu said. "I heard on the radio. A man called Maurice Traynor, they said. I had not known that his name was Maurice. What a dreadful thing to happen. You must be so shocked. You were, I know, his closest friend."

"I wasn't a friend of Traynor's," Bannister said with an unintended vehemence. "We were, of course, acquaintances," he went on, hoping that Abu hadn't noticed. "We met occasionally for a drink. But we were never close friends. I don't know why people assume that."

"My mistake."

The long lean face seemed to frown at him across the circular table. One could not be sure of the expression. It occurred to him that Abu was a dangerous man.

"What a shocking thing," Abu said again.

He could have had something to do with it, Bannister thought. He needn't have done it himself. He could have hired someone. It would not be difficult here to find a man who would kill. Perhaps it was easy anywhere for all he knew. He shifted, disconcerted, on his chair and watched Abu's frown fade away as if youth were returning to his face.

"You have no idea why it happened?"

"I wondered if you had?" Bannister said with a daring that surprised him.

Abu frowned again. "I don't quite know what you mean by that remark, Mr. Bannister."

"You mentioned some kind of scheme," Bannister blundered on. A sheep as a lamb, he thought. He was almost proud of his courage. "You said that Traynor and you made some money that way. You suggested that if I were interested..."

"Oh come now, Mr. Bannister." The gold teeth glinted and Bannister's pride went away. The moments were always too short to be counted of value. "You mean our system of betting?"

"Betting?"

"Mr. Traynor had worked out a system for horse-races. But it was not so very successful, I fear. I never believed that it would be. He wanted to start a syndicate, you understand the word?"

A waiter put a tall glass of gin and a bottle of tonic on the table. Bannister gave him a note and watched him fan the change across one side of the tray. That can't be true, he thought. As he took the awkward change he tried to remember how Abu had first mentioned the arrangement. Surely he had said that Traynor made money by giving him some kind of help? He thought that he remembered that. Or was the word assistance? He left some coins on the tray and saw the dangerous smile, the dark face watching with what one could imagine was menace.

"I see," he said, pouring some tonic into the glass, watching his fingers shaking. "You gave the impression that it was something more secret than that."

"I know that I did. I intended that. I didn't want any of my friends to be involved until we knew if the system was going to work. Why should you lose money?" The plausibility of the smile, the credibility of the words, surrounded Bannister like comfort. "Was that," he asked, "what he was doing in Casablanca?"

"I have no idea, Mr. Bannister. He never said anything to

136

me about Casablanca. Have you any idea when he returned? You didn't see him?"

"No."

"Strange. He must have arrived shortly before his death."

"I thought that there might be a connection," Bannister said.

"Well now you know that there is not. But I think, Mr. Bannister," the smile was now sympathetic, "that it might, perhaps, be as well if you did not mention this matter to anyone else. Or mention the kind of scheme. An unnecessary detail, don't you think?"

"Of course."

"I thought you would. Another drink, Mr. Bannister?"

"Thank you. I think I will."

He watched, unhappily, as Abu signalled for the waiter. Another initiative had gone. The betting scheme did not seem like the truth. He would keep on changing his mind. There was no certainty. "The scheme," he said. "How exactly did it work? Was it like . . . ?" He stopped and looked away. Abu was not listening. I could write to Stella, he thought, but the idea held no comfort.

"Don't cry," Señora Perez said.

"I can't help it."

"Ah, Mrs. Merton. I think", she said unexpectedly, "of you as if you were my very own daughter."

"It's shock, I suppose. Hearing about Mr. Traynor. And I'm really worried about Johnny. Suppose he's sick?"

"Sick? Sick! But look at him. He's well. Not sick, but well. How could you think he's sick?" She moved around the room like someone banishing spells, a small and friendly witch. "He's like a little saint."

"I'll bring him to the doctor," Janet said. "The English doctor in the square. Down near the market. He's always there in the evening."

"Yes, you could," Señora Perez said doubtfully. "Some-

137

times," she went on, "they are good. Sometimes they are bad."

Johnny was asleep in his cot. He seemed peaceful. The room was dim; Janet had closed the shutters. A cockroach moved uncertainly across the faded wall.

"I'm sorry that I cried. I don't know why I did. You've been very good to me."

She felt embarrassed by Señora Perez's emotion. The old woman seemed so strong and so helpless all at once. Some hair had come away from the parting and was falling raggedly across her face.

"I have not done anything."

"Even having someone to talk to . . ."

"You are lonely?"

"Well, sometimes I am."

"You have not heard from him yet?"

"No."

"Soon," Señora Perez said. "I know what it is to feel lonely. I have been lonely for many years now. Abdul I have and saints and God. They help me."

"I'm sure they do."

Perhaps there's kindness in her curiosity, Janet thought. She wants to help. Señora Perez stood there like a statue. Her immobility was almost shocking after so much movement.

"My husband went away," she said. "He was weak. A very, very weak man. He was never on the side with God."

She spoke without bitterness and calmly as if the words had no importance for her. She pushed back her hair. In the dim room her candour could not have been heightened by any emotion. "He wanted other women."

"I'm sorry."

It was always startling when people spoke so frankly about themselves. She remembered what Farrell had said about the man in Gibraltar. It was so much easier to see an image that had been created by oneself; the busy landlady, prying, losing

138

her temper in the steam-filled kitchen. One shied away from the dignity of other people's weakness.

"I tell you this to comfort you. You are young and have a husband to love. Your life is not over like my one is. To you the thought of death is far away. You do not think of it ever. You have your life and you have a baby."

She leaned over Johnny's cot and said, "A baby to love."

"But he may be sick," Janet said and the guilt and shame returned. It would be her fault if anything happened. Some part of the future depended on all that one did or did not do now. She looked at the baby and thought, Oh God, please . . . remembering Farrell's hand on her breast.

"You will not tell these things to any other."

"Of course not. I wouldn't ever. You've been so kind, Señora Perez."

"I would not like others to know."

"Nobody will know."

"I think that it might comfort you to hear. You have things to thank our God for."

"I know."

Janet wished that she were alone. She knew that Señora Perez would later regret having spoken. If David blamed her about Johnny. . . . He should have been here, she thought. He could be anywhere with anyone. He shouldn't have left me like this. He could say "I love you" so easily, too easily, she thought. It was always the same. He didn't seem to realize how difficult love could be. She would cry again if she weren't left alone now. "I don't want to keep you," she said. "I know that you have so much to do."

"I will say my prayer for your baby. You must pray. You must put your trust in our only God. He is mocked here. You must pray for Johnny to be well and he will be well. You have not being going to our church. Oh yes, I know, you say it is not my business." She accused her quietly across the room. "But if you did you would know what it can mean."

And be like you, Janet thought. No, that's unfair.

139

"I will," she said.

"Why should you not go there now? I will stay with Johnny."

"I couldn't leave him. Not now."

"You could. Look, he is sleeping, so peace. You will help him that way. By prayer."

"Maybe I will."

It would be nice to be away from the room and the guilt and worry about Johnny. It might even be nice to be in a church for a moment. She had listened to David's arguments and, without much difficulty, abandoned the familiar ritual. The first guilts went away quickly. One was not changed; one found that nothing changed. She thought that a faith that left one so unaffected when abandoned could hardly ever have been real. It had not saved Señora Perez from loneliness. It seemed to make no difference. Still, she thought, I'll go and see the church.

"The walk", she said, "will do me good."

The church was on a hill above the European town. She passed the office blocks, the motor bikes parked under leaning palm trees. Paris, she thought, must be a little like this, friendly and ordered and clean. I hope that Johnny is still asleep. She went along the Rue La Fontaine and saw the big American cars turn towards the Place d'Europe. Some would be going to Tetuan.

The church was very small. She blessed herself quickly in the porch. David had told her that the action had come from people's attempts to ward off evil spells. She felt ashamed as she knelt at the back of the church and looked towards the marble altar. This was one's childhood, recreated, the monstrous fears and hopes, the things that people had told her. The visit on All Souls' Day to pray for the souls of the dead, the candles before the shrines. The taste of the wafer on her tongue, the penitent's secret shames and fears. The statue that may have cried, the words in the hymns that one sang but did not understand. The *Tantum Ergo* and the priest carrying the Infant to the crib on Christmas morning. One betrayed it all by denial but to go back now would be a greater betrayal. If one did not believe one would only betray oneself by some kind of pretence. She thought, How could it be true? How could there be someone invisible who cares and looked towards the altar with the same old secret fear that somebody might be there. The Stations of the Cross pictured the dreadful story that had once seemed easy to believe. The words were in French. It's a missionary church, she thought, and an old priest dressed in a brown soutane came slowly from behind the altar. She could hear the creak of his sandals. He genuflected, then knelt before the Cross. She heard the whisper of his prayers, the occasional words emphasized like moans, the old sound of faith. I shouldn't have come here, she thought. The old fears were too confusing. It wasn't that one wondered again; it was simply that so many memories returned that one might not have lived since the last time one had knelt in a church. It means nothing. If it did I know that I'd care.

The priest held his arms out, imitating the figure on the Cross. He sighed and the whisper of his prayer continued. Does he believe? He'd have to, she thought. How terrible not to believe after living that kind of life. The bitterness would be too great to bear. To dedicate oneself to nothing at all in the only life that one had. She thought, It would be like being in love with someone and discovering he doesn't love you because he doesn't even exist. But David loves me. He couldn't say that he does so often if he didn't mean it. She watched the priest. He seemed to be as still, as dead, as unreal as the plaster Christ. A ray of light came suddenly through a stained glass window and fell across his shoulder. If that's faith, she thought, then perhaps it isn't really all that different from mine. I can't know for certain that David loves me but at least I can know that he exists. I can touch his body like Thomas is said to have touched the body of Christ. I can feel him in me. An insect crawled across the polished seat before the kneeling board. She watched its pointless journey with distaste then heard the creak of sandals. The priest came slowly towards her, reading his breviary. His face, she saw, was like the boneless face of some bad statue. She pretended to pray, covering her face with her hands. She could easily remember the words. "Remember, O most gracious Virgin Mary, that never was it known. . . ." The creak came slowly towards her. The words went on, unguided, through her mind. ". . . inspired with this confidence I fly unto thee, O Virgin of Virgins my mother." She took her hands away. The priest looked at her and smiled. His chin was blue from shaving. There was no confidence, no triumph, no faith, only friendliness in his smile. He could parody the crucifixion but the smooth, weak face bore no real signs of suffering. The taste of God in one's mouth was like paper, one stood and one sat as the altar boy clanged the bell. It left no trace. She heard his sandals on the tiled floor of the porch and decided to wait until he had gone. Johnny loved her.

"I love Johnny," she whispered, "I believe in Johnny," remembering him asleep in his cot. He had been baptized in Dublin. They had agreed to go through with the ritual; it could not do any harm. It was a convention; one was given one's name that way. It had nothing to do with belief. The board was hurting her knees. She would bring him to the doctor this evening. "There's no one there," she whispered as she looked at the altar. The stillness in the church seemed to prove her disbelief. And yet one feared a sign, some punishment. The nuns had warned that God was not mocked. If it were true, if there were really someone there, one drove in the iron nails and heard the gasps of pain, saw the broken, bleeding head. One cried in the crowd for Barabbas, turning one's face away from love.

God, she thought, if you're there be good to Johnny. It has nothing to do with him. This doubt, she knew, was probably the worst betrayal of all. One displayed a loveless selfishness. Denial was surely better, even more pleasing to God, if He existed and cared. He would not want a qualified love. And I won't offend you, she thought, an old and mean-

142

ingless phrase if one didn't believe in the rules of love and the price that one had to pay. Don't make him die. There's so much fever here and all kinds of disease. He's all that I have, she whispered into the empty stillness.

# Chapter Four

Farrell met Susan on the Avenue d'Espagne. He had almost forgotten her.

"Hello," she said. "I wondered if I'd see you again."

A blind man passed them, tapping the pavement with his stick. The sound was oddly plaintive. It seemed to express a kind of muted anger, Farrell thought, or rage.

"You're looking well," he said, noticing that she seemed much more relaxed.

"Well it's a great town isn't it? I'm really enjoying myself."

"Have you found a lot of excitement?"

"Sure. There's plenty of it."

Catherine's smile confronted him; her child would have smiled like that.

"And have you rubbed shoulders with celebrities?"

"Well not exactly," she said. "But I've met a lot of people. They're mostly American but there's a couple of British too. There's a colony here, you know?"

"Really?"

It was difficult to believe that he had ever cared about her. He wondered why he had wanted her. It was, he supposed, the smile, the image.

"Yes, I thought you'd be interested," she said. "They're mostly creative writers. Poets," she said with triumph. "You should come along some time. They meet in a place called the Silver Bear. It's a café. I'll tell you how to get there."

"Would you like a cup of coffee?"

"Thanks."

They walked to a pavement café. She said, "I'd prefer a Coke if that's okay." They sat down, side by side and he ordered, looking across at the dusty palm trees and the people coming back from the beach.

"And how have you being doing?" she asked.

"Taking it easy."

She drank the Coke through a straw.

"No excitement at all?"

He shook his head. "Or no celebrities either," he said. She laughed.

"Maybe that's the way you want it," she said. "Is it?"

"I don't seem to have much choice."

"So come along some evening, won't you? I think you'd like it there. There's a boy from Chicago called Barrow. He told me he once met Kerouac. He writes the same kind of way. He's a kind of screwball," she said, with what might have been tenderness. "But he's got a lot of talent. I've read a few of his stories."

Her enthusiasm made him feel tired. He nodded as she told him how to get to the café.

"I'll do that some evening," he said.

"You'll find it stimulating."

"I'm sure that I will."

He knew that he would not. It was exactly the kind of place that he made a point of avoiding in Dublin.

"Talking about excitement," she said. "You heard about the murder."

"Where?"

"Right here in town. It happened this morning I guess." The last of her drink gurgled noisily as she sucked at it through the straw. "Ed Barrow told me on the 'phone. He heard it somewhere. Some Englishman called Traynor was knifed."

"You're sure that his name was Traynor?"

"Pretty sure. Knifed in the neck, Ed said. You think you know somebody?"

"Not really."

If she had the name right it could hardly be coincidental.

"You didn't hear any other details?"

"No." She frowned. "I think Ed might have told me the

name of the street. But I forget it now. But I'm pretty sure of the man's name. You know a Traynor?"

Farrell drank his coffee. "Just the name," he said. "I heard it somewhere recently I think." A gull cried from the branches of a tree and she said, "I'd better go. I have a date to meet a friend."

"I'll see you in the Silver Bear."

Watching her walk away he wondered why anyone should have killed a man like Traynor. He thought of the coats in the wardrobe. Their respectability seemed so far from violence. It could not have been much of a life that left so very little behind; some coats, an old rolled newspaper, dust and a debt to Señora Perez. He left coins on the table and went back to the house. The cat came padding down the stairs. He knocked at Janet's door. Señora Perez opened it.

"Yes, Mr. Farrell?"

"I'm looking for Mrs. Merton, Señora."

"She's not here."

"You don't know where she is?"

The old woman smiled. "I do," she said triumphantly. "She went to pray. You look at me surprised, Mr. Farrell?"

"Oh, not at all," he said. He could see that Johnny was asleep.

"You don't know when she'll be back?"

"I mind the baby for her. You see."

She smiled again as if happy about the evasion.

"I'll try for her later," Farrell said.

She seemed to be disappointed that he had no more questions to ask. She wiped her hands on her apron then brushed hair back from her face. "I understand. There is another thing, Mr. Farrell." The smile had dwindled away. Her face seemed shrunken and her eyes, he saw, were bloodshot. "There has been such a trouble here."

"Is Mrs. Merton all right?"

"Yes, but that Mr. Traynor was killed. You come in here a minute."

She beckoned him into the room and closed the door.

146

She spoke very softly. "We must not waken the baby. Yes, some Arabs they killed poor Mr. Traynor. The police were here in my house. An Inspector. . . ." She had raised her voice, then, glancing uneasily at the cot, she whispered, "He insulted me this Inspector."

"But where did Traynor die?" Farrell said. "It didn't happen here, did it?"

"Not here. Two streets away."

"And Mrs. Merton is safe?"

"Why Mrs. Merton all the time? Why would not she be safe?"

"I just thought when I saw you here . . ."

"Mrs. Merton was worried. It made her think this baby might be sick." She brushed the thought away impatiently and Farrell felt a sudden shame that someone else's death should seem so unimportant.

"What did the police say, Señora?"

"I told you. That Inspector. Pagan. He insult me." The anger in her whisper and the way that she stood there, looking for redress, showed that she was not mourning. At least I didn't know him, Farrell thought. But a violent death should shock one more than this. He saw a cockroach move across the flaking wall. Señora Perez said, "And he ask me questions. Who was in my house? You were not here when he come. He talk with Mr. Bannister. He said", she added angrily, "that he come back."

"Well that's quite natural," Farrell said. "They'd want to know of course . . ."

"What know in my house?"

"Traynor *did* live here."

"Then he search your room. I could not make him stop. He search."

This is probably how it matters, Farrell thought. How did it change one's plans? Was one affected? Death was not important but its probable consequences troubled one. Traynor became a symbol of disruption. It was difficult to feel real grief. One knew that one should at times and simulated it, ashamed that it was not there. Would this make any difference with Janet? The police would be around the house. He looked at her bed and saw that the towel from the beach was lying on the floor. Desire came like a depression; her breast pressing against his hand, the taste of salt on her lips. He said, "It doesn't matter. He'd naturally search that room."

"It does matter in my house."

"You can ask for a warrant", he suggested.

"Warren?" she said. "Why would I ask warren? What warren to do?" Her English seemed to desert her. She muttered in Spanish and the baby woke and started to cry.

"Now listen." Señora Perez pointed a shaking finger towards the sound. "What good is warren now," she said, "with trouble and trouble? A warren! Now what use warren?"

The crying annoyed him as much as the meaningless question. If Janet were here, he thought, she'd do something. But the baby was there like proof of her love for another man.

"I'll go upstairs," he said. Señora Perez was fussing around the cot, making sounds to the baby who cried up at her, relentlessly. "I'll see Mrs. Merton later."

He left with some relief and went to his room. He would not have guessed that anyone had been there. Its bare familiarity seemed unchanged. The coats were in the wardrobe. His suitcase, he saw, was at the bottom of the bed and a paperback book was lying on the floor where he had left it. He could hear the baby's wails and Señora Perez's voice imploring it to be quiet. It had been a much more professional search than the last one. There was, perhaps, less to fear. Now that Traynor was dead there would probably be an explanation for the attack. He lay on the bed. The sun had burned one shoulder. In some way or other, he thought, that bar and Durcan are involved in whatever has happened. And the pedlar on the beach. Janet said that he's always there. Desire for her body distracted him like pain. He shifted to take some weight from the tingling shoulder and noticed that the house was quiet. The crying had seemed invincible; the quietness was like victory.

He was asleep when the Inspector came.

"I will not keep you long, Mr. Farrell. If you have your passport here . . ."

"Certainly. You didn't find it this morning?"

"I made no serious attempt to do so, Mr. Farrell. I knew that you would be here now." He looked at the passport. "Ireland," he said. "I never saw one like this one before." He put it in his pocket. "I will return it to you soon. Can you tell me anything about Mr. Traynor? I am certain that you heard the sad news."

"I've never even met him."

"How interesting. But perhaps you know some thing about him. It is written on your passport that you are a journalist." He smiled slowly and disarmingly. "Is it a big coincidence, Mr. Farrell, that you happen to be here? Staying in Mr. Traynor's room?"

"An unpleasant coincidence."

"It certainly could not be very pleasant. You will write an article for your newspaper?"

"I might."

"Not stupid article I hope. The tourist trade is important to Morocco. We welcome every tourist. You admire our King, Mr. Farrell? A very good man. He is very widely admired."

"If I knew", Farrell said, "what happened in Casablanca in 1965 . . ."

"He has done such good work for our country. Social policy. And just look at this town. After years of division . . ."

"One hears that the secret police . . ."

"Oh now really, Mr. Farrell. You have been reading your colleagues. They can be very silly. There seemed to be no limit to their invention. We have, of course, internal security. Do you tell me that your Ireland has not got so?"

"I hardly threaten that security, Inspector."

"Indeed you do not, Mr. Farrell. Neither am I very secret. I am sure that you do not use heroin."

"Do I look as if I do?"

"One can not always tell, Mr. Farrell, by looking. Except at the arms, of course."

"You can look if you like."

The Inspector seemed mildly embarrassed. "A mere formality," he said. Farrell pulled up the sleeves of his shirt. "You have been most helpful, Mr. Farrell. I do not think that there is anything else. If you want information for anything you write I can put you in touch with some people."

"I'll keep that in mind."

"It is a great mistake, Mr. Farrell, to think that Western democracy, in the way that you understand it, is the only form of good government. We live in an old civilization, much older, Mr. Farrell, than in most European countries. Older than Ireland, I'm sure. There are different ways of ruling. Some journalists show a surprising ignorance of history. I must not disturb your siesta any more." He opened the door and stood there like a friendly waiter. "If you hear anything that I should know, Mr. Farrell."

"If I think it might interest you, Inspector, I'll let you know."

"Please let me judge that. Your friend Mrs. Merton. I have not been able to see her. How nice that her husband is away."

"I don't think I follow you, Inspector."

"I am a man of the world, Mr. Farrell. Is not that the expression that I should use? A man of the world. I believe that she is a beautiful woman. You do not know her husband, no?"

"I don't see the point."

"Must there be one, Mr. Farrell? I am having conversation with you." The smile was still disarming. He brushed his lapel with his fingers. "I will not interfere in your affairs if you think that you can assist me with mine. Thank you for your help so far. I feel that we know each other now. This understanding. A beautiful woman, Mrs. Merton, I believe. Her husband is hardly wise. In another country and the sun. These things will happen, Mr. Farrell."

150

"Nothing has happened, Inspector."

"Not yet, Mr. Farrell."

He felt only mild resentment.

"I hope that you get better evidence for Traynor's death."

"Oh I will, Mr. Farrell. I am efficient. I can be a very good friend." The plausible voice went on like the smile; both must have been carefully rehearsed.

"Have you a theory about Traynor?"

"Not a theory, no. A feeling, perhaps, yes certainly a feeling. Here we sometimes think that theories matter less than feelings, Mr. Farrell. I knew Mr. Traynor a little bit. And we have, of course, a record of some time ago. He was not a very happy man. He was homosexual. Did you know that? Yes. But another time we can talk about these things. Please think of ways that you can help me, Mr. Farrell. You will not regret them. I am a discreet man."

He's a rather foolish man, Farrell thought, but he could be a bloody nuisance. The Inspector's voice came, muffled, from the stairs. He may succeed in scaring Janet. His suspicion could be there creating guilt and complications like a picture of her husband or the baby's cry.

"Are you in there, Mr. Farrell?"

"Yes, Señora."

"I will come in."

She looked around the room as if expecting to find the Inspector there.

"When you came", she said, "I told you about this." She held out a picture in a heavy frame.

"It's very nice."

"He is the Holy Infant of Prague. Your Mr. Traynor took him down from the wall. How could that be luck? The Infant, he blessed the room." She polished the glass on the picture vigorously. The Infant was painted pink and silver like a circus clown. A smug smile puffed out his face and a heavy crown was balanced on his head.

"Most lovely thing," Señora Perez said. "An art. I have

had him for many, many years. His place is on that wall. I said so to Mr. Traynor. He was foolish."

"I'll help you put him back if you like. Is Mrs. Merton downstairs?"

"No. She come back and then went to the doctor with her baby. You hold him please. Now look, the nail is here. I tell you, Mr. Farrell, God will bless this room now."

# Chapter Five

"Perfectly healthy. A really bonny baby." The doctor was trying to please her. "You must look after him well," he said. "He really is in tip-top shape." Above his head a faded sepia picture of a college group was hanging crookedly. He winced at his fingers; a faint smell of whisky lingered around the desk.

"I'm so glad to hear it. I was a bit worried."

"Well I can assure you that you needn't have been."

"He seemed a bit flushed."

"Just good health, Mrs. Merton. The fine bloom of youth. Would that all of us had it."

"I'm sorry to have wasted your time."

"But, dear lady, you haven't. I assure you you mustn't think that. You're perfectly right to insist on the very best medical care. One can't take these chances, you know. Little fellows like Jimmy here need constant checking. They do. You must take the right precautions, as you do, Mrs. Merton."

"Another child I know", Janet said, "seemed ill."

"And that naturally worried you. Of course. If everyone had your attitude, Mrs. Merton, the world would be a healthier place." He picked up a pencil and tapped it impatiently against his unshaven chin. If he looked more reliable . . . Janet thought. But he was good before, he gave me the right medicine. The collar of his shirt was stained with flecks of blood. "So you needn't worry any more. This climate must suit him," he said. "As it seems to suit you. I'm quite partial to heat myself. You look better every time," he added with a tired gallantry. "It's always a pleasure to see you. And little Jimmy." He chewed the end of his pencil. "But he is getting rather big for carrying. You must get him a pram, Mrs. Merton. They're excellent things. You could strain yourself you know . . ."

"As soon as we get back. To Europe."

"Don't leave it too long though, will you?" He smiled with big, carious teeth. His face was unusually pale. She stood up, taking the baby in her arms. "You heard about Mr. Traynor?" she said, remembering what Señora Perez had told her. It had not seemed so very important then.

"Traynor? I don't believe I've seen him for some months, no. Poor fellow, I suppose that's a good sign. He's beginning to cope with his complaints. They're largely psychosomatic you know but of course they're perfectly real to Traynor. It happens to fellows abroad. Especially us bachelors, you see. We have much too much free time. We brood, Mrs. Merton."

He was incredulous when she told him about the murder.

"But I simply can't believe it. The man was inoffensive to a fault." He blinked at her, bewildered. Surprise had brought some colour to his face. She could picture him reaching for the whisky bottle as soon as she had gone. His hand was shaking as he took out his handkerchief to wipe his sweating forehead. She felt a strong repulsion.

"I quite liked him," he said. "The poor fellow was rather decent. A bit of a bore, of course. He would go on about the army and that kind of thing but he was never the least offensive. I think he pictured himself as some kind of hero, you see. Harmless poor fellow." He opened the door for her.

"I don't suppose you know about the funeral . . ." he said. The dirty handkerchief was hanging from his hand like the flag of some past surrender.

"I haven't heard."

"It's at times like this", he said, "that one feels rather helpless, don't you think? If one were at home the procedure is perfectly clear. One attends the service and that kind of thing but here . . . well, they tend not to do the same things. Yes I still fear death," he said as if answering a question that she had asked. "My colleagues used to laugh but there it is. I can't help it, I'm too dedicated to health. One broods when one lives alone. Traynor was a decent poor fellow." He looked down the street at some children who were playing with a

154

ball made from paper and string. "All this squalor," he said. "One can never hope to belong. I suppose that one doesn't want to. And one isn't wanted. They dislike Europeans, you see. One comes here with such hope then finds that there's nothing but sadness and failure. I think I'd prefer cremation," he said more brightly. "It's clean, don't you think, and decent? A good way to go when you have to. Not like lying in a coffin. That's much too accurate a reflection of life to please me. All that decay of cells. The endless waste of living. They all go into the dark. Eliot, isn't it? I'm pleased to see you, Mrs. Merton. That's a beautiful fellow you've got there. Little Jimmy."

"Johnny. And you're sure?"

"Oh indeed, indeed, most healthy. Good-day to you now."

She walked past the children. The ball was coming apart; shreds of paper littered the street. "You *are* heavy," she said to Johnny. His eyes were closed. She noticed, with tenderness, the veins across the lids. They seemed too delicate to have any purpose.

Poor Salim, she thought with guilt. I'm sure that he's better by now. It has not been prayer. There had been nothing wrong to put right. One reverted to childhood in stress, an escape to beliefs that meant nothing for most of the time. They returned to one with fear not love. There was no conviction, no trust; one felt a kind of uneasiness in the dark. Her mother had believed fiercely as her father came stumbling through the door. The sounds had been part of martyrdom. She should have left him, Janet thought. Or maybe he should have gone. It was a belief in God that had held them together and made them turn towards hate. And God accepted hate as He accepted pain if it were offered to Him in prayer. He accepted anything; such callousness could not be comprehended. People swallowed Him and went on hating. A statue cried in Galway. She had seen the queue outside the Dominican church, hoping to see a tear, waiting for the sign of sadness that would prove the existence of love. Her mother had brought her there, away from the holiday beach

155

in Salthill and the slot-machines in Tofts. They had not seen a miracle. The statue had been removed. It was, a priest explained, some condensation that had caused the tears. The statue was only a shabby piece of plaster. "I wonder, I wonder," her mother had said as they went towards the bus-stop in Eyre Square. "It could be true. They mightn't be pretending for some reason. But it could be true like Lourdes. A sign." She had wanted too much to believe.

Janet could see her face now, surprisingly young, but her eyes had been damaged by life, by the hate and the hope that made her turn for love to a statue shedding tears. It was an easy escape. One could believe so easily in anything but one-self; believe in the love of a child or of a husband who was not there. Or one could believe in Farrell. I know that he wants me, she thought. Pleasure was always real.

A girl wearing jodhpurs came from one of the hotels. "Oh for Christ's sake," she called, "he's not here. The stupid bugger!"

"Well I told him to be."

"You know what he's bloody well like!"

"Never mind, pet. He'll find it I'm sure."

The voice of the man seemed practised in reassurance.

"Well I'm not going to wait here for long."

She looked at Janet. Her angry, beautiful face was some-thing to be envied. Emotions so easily expressed must be easy to throw aside. "He can go and stuff himself if he's not here soon. Really . . ."

The man had appeared. He looked casually down the street.

"Let's give him a minute or two."

Janet passed them. The baby seemed heavier than before. It's not fair. Such a burden, she thought, and the girl's voice followed her.

"But isn't he a proper bastard!"

"Oh come on now, take it easy, Jill."

"On a day like today of all days. That bloody sun . . ."

If you had to carry Johnny, Janet thought, you'd know all

about the sun. She should have asked the doctor for a bill. That was two calls she owed for now. She would have to change the last traveller's cheque very soon. Money would be the next problem. If one could shout on the pavement the relief would be immense. Shout like that girl; not like Farrell's man in Gibraltar or the woman who stood near Parnell's statue in Dublin and roared at the passing cars. The eyes of the mad reproached one. They focused on some kind of truth that was outside one's view. The mad had a secret. But that girl was sane and spoiled and could do exactly what she liked. "You're far too heavy," she said, "but you're well," and felt too tired to be resentful. She wondered again about Salim. I should go down there now to see. I can cut down this way.

A narrow, tree-lined avenue went down towards the beach. Just to see how he is. I won't go in and risk . . . just to see.

A small, white sports car roared past; she could see the girl's face, transformed by laughter.

It isn't fair. No one would ever believe that he left me here like this. If he didn't trust me he wouldn't have left me at all. She was penalized for being faithful. And can he be trusted? For all I know his research could be about how they do it in the mountains. Making notes when he sleeps with them. She walked down the avenue: a heat-haze shimmered on the pavement. A policeman seemed to stare at her with interest. I doubt it. I suppose he's faithful too. Does he even like it much? When he doesn't like it it isn't my fault. I want him.

The success of their love-making varied more than she would ever have believed to be possible. Sometimes he wanted her fiercely, thrusting into her as if seeking escape from himself. At other times they went through the movements and her own body sensed the dull disinterest in his. She had looked for a pattern; happiness, arguments, drink, but had been unable to find one.

The policeman was walking on the opposite side of the avenue, matching his steps to her own. His khaki uniform

157

was worn and stained. He could be following me, she thought. Don't be ridiculous. What would the police care? Could it have something to do with Mr. Traynor? She hesitated for a moment, the baby clenched tightly in her arms. I wish that you weren't called Johnny. It was a silly name, inadequate for all that he could be. They had chosen it casually. She looked across at the policeman who seemed to smile as if they had come to some agreement. I'm not just something to be stared at, she thought with bitterness. I'm letting things get on my nerves. David said that I was too sentimental she thought, remembering the shame that she had felt at the time. It did not seem to matter now.

The policeman was no longer opposite her. She could hear his footsteps but he seemed to be lagging behind. This isn't my day, she thought, and you, you rascal. . . . The baby stirred in her arms. She crossed the Avenue d'Espagne and waited for a train to shudder slowly past. Johnny watched it but did not cry. He was accustomed to the noise and the steam and the shouts of the driver. The open carriages were piled with logs and rusty, dented oil-drums.

The beach was still crowded. She felt no affinity with the girls there. They were not real. It seemed unlikely that they could understand the kind of life that she had. They would not accept it. She heard their laughter as if it were talk in another language. The boys who sometimes mocked her were standing near two elderly women sitting stolidly on a rug. She walked along to the café. The door was closed, the shutters were across on the windows. She knocked on the door.

"There's no one in there."

"I'm sorry?"

"There isn't anyone in there. The owner's baby died. I was sitting here when it happened." The old man was in his shirt-sleeves. He sat in the shade of the café wall, a camera beside him on the sand, his coat stretched neatly on a newspaper, his toes poking up at the sky from his brown leather sandals. "It was quite an experience, you know. I don't want to sound callous, of course. I'm sorry and that but it was a novel experience. I had just nodded off to sleep." He cleared his throat and spat noisily on the sand. "I beg your pardon. It's phlegm, you see. I'm not as young as I was. That's my daughter," he said, pointing vaguely towards the sea. "She made me come on this holiday. To tell you the truth I'd rather have stayed at home. But she insisted. The sun will do you good, she said. Such nonsense. I spend all day avoiding it. Burns me to buggery. Is that your baby? He's a nice little fellow. What's his name?"

"How do you know that the baby died?"

"The other one? But my dear child, such commotion. Never heard the likes in my life. I hope I'm not sounding callous. I wouldn't want that. I felt really sorry for the mother. Pretty little thing. Did you know her? She sold soft drinks and ice-cream and that sort of thing. Used to wander in there myself, for the sake of the shade." He spat again with total self-assurance and wiped his mouth with the back of his hand. "I heard the crying," he said. "Never heard anything like it before. Moans and wails and that. You'd think it was the end of the world. Didn't know what to do. How in hell would I? Next thing they came trooping out. The baby was under her arm like a parcel. A most extraordinary thing to see. A couple of other women were with her. I tried to take a photograph. I doubt that I got it, though." He squinted up at her, his face flushed with excitement. "No time to fiddle with the thing," he said. "The meter and that. A pity. It would have been good if I got it."

"Where did they go?"

"Towards the town. Don't understand their ways here, do you? I suppose they bury them like anyone else."

She walked back across the beach. If I start to cry . . . she thought. There were tears in her eyes. I won't stop. She would cry for Johnny and David and for herself. She would even cry for Salim, perhaps for Traynor. But the doctor said you were healthy. You couldn't just die like that. Not the way that I've minded you. The smell of marijuana came from somewhere near and gulls protested. She should find the woman who was not much older than herself and say that she was sorry for her trouble. But would that make the slightest difference? It would not make him live again or make Johnny any more safe. It could not have been prayer; it could not have been superstition. His mother must have prayed as well. It was vaccinations and proper care and food and love. She must have loved her baby. She must have loved him and done her very best. I'd have wailed and broken his stupid camera.

She crossed the railway line.

"You Mrs. Merton?"

The policeman smiled and raised his eyebrows to emphasize the question.

"You?" he said pointing at her, "Mrs. Merton?"

"What's wrong?"

"Yes, you are. Here please."

He nodded towards a car that was parked near by.

"Talk, please, with Inspector. You."

She followed him towards the car.

"Is there something wrong? I saw you following me earlier . . ."

"No you," he said smiling. A man in the back of the car opened a door.

"I am a police Inspector, Mrs. Merton. We could talk, perhaps, for some minutes. Will you sit in here? You must be tired. That's a big baby that you have to carry."

She stood at the door of the car. "I don't understand," she said.

"Just some questions, Mrs. Merton. No need to worry, I assure you. You could help me a little. Do you fear", he asked, "some kind of kidnap? But look." He waved his hand expansively around the car. "No driver. It can not go anywhere by itself. I really think that you would be more comfortable but if you would prefer . . ."

"Is it something to do with David?"

"David. Tell me about David."

160

"Is there something wrong?"

"With David? But who is David?"

"My husband."

"Ah, your husband. No, no, I'm sure that he's perfectly well. It's a question about a man called Traynor."

"Oh Mr. Traynor," she said with relief.

"Exactly. You heard about Mr. Traynor?"

"I heard that he had been killed. And the baby," she said. "The baby died." She felt the tears on her cheeks before she realized that she was crying. "I'm sorry."

"Please, please. You must not be upset." He got out of the car. "Do sit in and rest," he said, holding the door open. "You are tired."

"It was only a little baby."

She got into the car. The Inspector spoke in Arabic and the policeman walked away.

"We can have a talk," the Inspector said, sitting on the seat beside her.

Johnny looked around the car. He touched the back of the seat with his fingers and smiled.

"May I offer you a handkerchief?"

"No thanks. I'm sorry," she said. "I thought . . ." She wiped her face with her hand. "I thought it was something else. And the baby upset me. He was only Johnny's age."

"That café on the beach that you went to . . ."

"His mother owned it."

"Whose mother?"

"The baby who died."

"I understand what you mean." The Inspector opened a packet of cigarettes. "Someone reported to me that a child had died. From suffocation, I think."

"Not from suffocation!"

"No? I could, of course, be wrong. You will smoke?"

"No thank you."

"Please excuse me if I do. If you would please open that other window. . . . You knew this baby that died?"

"To see."

"To see. And how about Mr. Traynor? How well did you know him?"

The smoke from his cigarette curled slowly past her eyes.

"Not well," she said.

Johnny reached for the smoke, laughing at the back of his throat, trying to catch it in his fingers. She stroked the top of his head and felt her love for him bring on more tears. She said, "I knew him to see as well. Just to say hello to."

"You are Irish, Mrs. Merton?"

The Inspector's face was oddly round, she noticed. He had pimples on his chin.

"Yes I am. From Dublin."

"And your husband?"

"He's from England."

"And Mr. Farrell?"

"Mr. Farrell's from Ireland"

"You are lovers, yourself and Mr. Farrell?"

She stopped stroking Johnny's head and looked at the smooth, round face.

"Who told you that?" she said. "You've no right . . ."

"Please, Mrs. Merton. I assure you. I would not be offensive. I am a man of the world. I am discreet. When I spoke to Mr. Farrell . . ."

"He couldn't have told you that."

"Not exactly. But the way that he spoke . . ."

"I met him yesterday for the very first time. Do you think that I'm some kind of whore?"

She was crying again, ashamed of the stupid tears. The Inspector seemed sympathetic. He shook his head and stared, as if with embarrassment, through the open window. "Oh no," he said. He turned to her. "I must apologize if I have offended you. I assure you that was not my intention. I merely thought . . . perhaps a small affair. Your husband is away. I mention it only because someone heard voices from your room on the night that Mr. Traynor was murdered. You understand", he said persuasively, "how edges must be tied. All things must be explained." The persuasive voice went on through the circling smoke.

"I don't see what business," she said. "It's my business." Johnny looked with wonder at her tears and reached to touch them. She moved her head away. He clenched his face, getting ready to cry. "Little fellow," she said, "don't you start," taking his hand and shaking it to distract him. "You've no right", she said, "to pry."

"I agree. But forgive me. It cannot be described as prying. You must attempt to understand. It's important to know all movements in the house on that night. Who was in your room, Mrs. Merton? Your husband has not returned?"

"No. It was Mr. Farrell."

"Is that a little unusual?"

"It's not illegal, is it?"

"I agree." He spoke with exaggerated patience. "You're quite free to entertain as you please. Within certain limits, of course." He smiled. "It is just that you said . . ."

"We were talking."

"That is quite possible, I agree. But", he smiled again, looking directly into her eyes, shrugging his shoulders, "not everyone would believe it. Forgive me, but human nature . . ."

"We talked for a while."

"What did you talk about?"

"I forget. Nothing important."

"Nothing about Mr. Traynor?"

"No. Why should we?"

"Perhaps you have forgotten the details. Your memory", he said, "by your own admission is not so very good. It would not be unusual to talk about Mr. Traynor. He was a resident in the house."

"We didn't."

"You can be quite sure of that?" He threw his cigarette butt out on to the street and started to examine his nails. "And how about Mr. Bannister?"

"He wasn't there."

"I did not suggest that you gave a party, Mrs. Merton.

Was Mr. Bannister a very close friend of Mr. Traynor, do you think?"

"I have no idea."

"You are a very vague lady, Mrs. Merton."

"I'm tired," she said. The tears had dried on her face. She knew that they must look ugly but she did not care. "There's too much death," she said.

"That is an interesting observation. I quite agree with you there. You had not met Mr. Farrell at any time before?"

"I told you I hadn't."

"Did you? I have no memory of that. However. The coincidence of both of you coming from Ireland. Mr. Traynor you would have last seen when?"

"Weeks ago," she said. "Señora Perez said he'd gone to Casablanca."

"Really? There would, I suppose, be no reason to believe that your husband had gone there with him?"

"They didn't even know each other," she said. He stared at her impassively, his fingers bent, his thumbs pressing busily against cuticles. She said, "You're trying to make a mystery out of everything."

"That is not my intention. I want to simplify things. To take the mystery out of them."

"I must go now," she said. "Johnny should be in bed."

"That other baby? Had you any special reason for being upset?"

"He's dead!"

"How many babies do you think, Mrs. Merton, die in this city every year?"

"That's not the point. I knew him. I knew his mother," she said. "And he died. Wouldn't that upset you?"

"To be frank, it would not, unless I had fathered it, of course."

"Well it upset me!"

He smiled. "You are tender-hearted," he said. "It is a quality that I admire. British women bore me usually, Mrs. Merton. They are so brash, do you think?"

"You don't want to ask me any more questions, do you?"

"Do you want to give me any answers?"

"I don't suppose you know where she lived? The woman in the café. Salim's mother. I'd like to visit her", she said, "and see if there's anything that I can do."

"You can do nothing. She will have her own people."

She found that she was crying again. Impatiently, she said, "It's so stupid. I don't know why . . ."

"Who have you got to do things for you, Mrs. Merton?"

"I don't need anyone," she said, wishing that David were back. "I don't need anyone."

"Perhaps you are not the best judge of that," he said, putting his hand heavily on her knee. It lay there like a weight, a piece of brown and puffy flesh. It might have been entirely lifeless. Johnny looked at it and touched it uneasily with his foot. She said, "Please take it away."

He did so and smiled at her warmly.

"Of course. A friendly gesture."

She reached for the handle of the door.

"Allow me to drive you to your house."

"I'd prefer to walk."

"Now that is very foolish, Mrs. Merton. You should travel there in the car. Why walk and make yourself more tired?"

"I'd prefer to," she said. The handle of the door was difficult to reach. "I'd prefer to. Now let me go."

"You do not want to walk through the streets when your face is covered with tears. Such a pity to see you crying." Holding Johnny in one arm, she pushed at the warm, chrome handle. "I can manage all right by myself."

"So I see, Mrs. Merton. For how long more, I wonder, will you have to do just that?"

"I don't have to answer your questions. I'm sure you could be reported," she said. "To someone. You've done nothing at all but upset me. You have no right at all to insult me. You made me sit here in the car. You knew that I didn't want to. If my husband knew!"

He smiled and Johnny started to cry. She hated both of

them; the round, smiling face and the small one, twisted into ugly protest. "Oh please," she said to neither of them, "please." She got out of the car, clumsily, hitting her knee against the side of the door. "Please!" Johnny shrieked. His face was red and swollen with what could have been adult rage.

"Are you sure, Mrs. Merton?" The Inspector's face looked up at her quizzically. "I will be glad to drive you there."

She walked away quickly, joining a group of people who were going back to some hotel. A woman looked at her and said something. She did not hear what it was. Johnny cried against her breasts, gulping, his fists hitting her shoulder again and again.

Please, she thought, please, please, please, not noticing that people were staring at her.

# Chapter Six

Farrell wished that he had waited for Janet. He drank his iced mint tea and looked at a week-old copy of the *Daily Express* that someone had left on the floor beside the table: some pictures of Vietnam, a starlet in a bathing suit. He put it back on the floor and finished his tea.

He hoped that there was nothing wrong with Johnny. She must have been very worried. He should have stayed with Señora Perez, admiring the holy picture. A waiter said, "Any more?" "No thanks," he said. "I'm going soon."

The waiter limped away towards a dark, cool corner like an injured animal who hopes to escape from pain. There was no one else in the café. A small fan whirred erratically above the door and an Arab poster on the wall lifted a little from the draught.

He wanted to see that bar near the docks and try to remember what had been said about Traynor. He remembered the waiter's face and the exaggerated toughness of his talk as if he had learned to speak by watching reel after reel of old, bad films. Someone called Durcan had shouted from upstairs; the abusive voice had been as deadly as the heat. There had been a dog there and the barman had said, "I could tell you about Traynor." Was that it? He lighted a cigarette and watched the poster move against the wall. It could be like yesterday, he thought, and the waste of chasing that man through the town. He had felt so foolish. He said, "I'll have another glass of mint tea please," and the waiter came from the corner, carrying a glass as if he had known all the time that it would be wanted.

"Thank you."

He paid and drank it quickly. If there was anything wrong with Johnny, he would get no nearer to her. She would certainly let the demands of the baby win. He left the café. It was much cooler in the street; the sky was taking on the light green shade of evening. He walked past the merchants' stalls; the smell of leather and meat and charcoal-burning beneath the skewers of kebab. A young man whittled a piece of wood with a knife, carving a small, crude camel. The long blade cut curling slivers away from the pointed, irregular hump. He should buy her a present. He looked at a tray of trinkets, some dresses hanging from a stall. He did not know what she liked. He knew almost nothing about her. A fat woman held up a dress and waved it, signalling at him. The imitation silk shone like the feathers of a bird, preening itself in courtship. He could not imagine her wearing it.

He came to the top of the steps. Below, across the rooftops, he could see the docks and the dark green stretch of sea. He walked down past the tinsmith's stall and came to the narrow street where the bar was. Some children were playing outside it. I needn't ask any questions there, he thought. I'll just order a drink and listen.

The children seemed to be playing some kind of hopscotch. He thought with resentment of Johnny. The child could cry his way between them like a warning, demanding all of her love. She would have to think about David and marriage and responsibility. He remembered her tears. She had cried from such loneliness, her baby sleeping near by in the cot that was like some sort of cage. When women cried, he thought, they bore a strange resemblance to each other as if grief were the common factor of the heart. And Johnny could make her cry until she would be like Catherine and himself, vulnerable to anything but love. He watched the children playing, resenting their enthusiasm, their ignorance of grief. Their vitality accused him across the narrow street. He stood with his hands in his pockets, half-hidden in the shade of a doorway, reluctant to go into the bar. He could hear the gulls from the pier. The sound of the tinsmith's hammer came down the wide stone steps, a steady tick. I'm being foolish again, he thought, this kind of indecisiveness is pointless. A long, black car came slowly down the street and stopped outside the bar. Farrell stepped back into the doorway and watched. The Inspector got out of the car. He said something to the children and smiled with satisfaction as they ran away. One of them turned and made a gesture but he did not notice; he was locking the car. He went into the bar and Farrell heard someone shouting up to Durcan before the door swung shut. It was something more than coincidence. If I had been in there, he wondered, what would he have said? What questions would he have asked? He looked across at the door, expecting it to open, wondering what he should do. The street was empty; only the tinsmith's hammer gave indication of life. He felt exposed and foolish, standing without any purpose in a doorway. If he sees me here that will look even more suspicious, he thought, but he did not want to go away. He pressed back as closely as he could against the door and waited.

He had once followed an Irish politician for two days, waiting in the doorway of a small antique shop near the Dail for the man's black Hillman to appear. He remembered, with a sense of shame, the innocent routine that he had witnessed; the lunches in the Saddle Room with a girl who, on checking, he found to be the man's own daughter, the drinks in the bar of Power's Hotel. The reason for the assignment had never been explained. He had driven around for two days, following the car and eavesdropping in bars and shops, waiting pointlessly outside the Dail and watching the bedroom light go out in a dark, suburban road. Ever since then he could not see a picture of the man without recalling some of the shame.

A small car drove past; a GB plate was fixed to its boot. He watched the dust spurt dryly from beneath its wheels. A hooter sounded down at the docks, a hollow, plaintive note. He looked at his watch. She must be back from the doctor by now. He would go to her room and ask how Johnny was, feigning pleasure or concern. Involvement made one a hypocrite. He wanted her far too much to risk being honest. Even love demanded such duplicity. If this door opens, he thought,

I'll fall back into somebody's arms. There was, he guessed, a courtyard behind and he thought that he could hear the splash of a fountain. He sneezed and reached for a handkerchief as the Inspector came out of the bar. He watched the car drive away. The Inspector had not seen him. It stopped near the end of the street. A man in a green shirt came from a doorway and got into the passenger seat. The car turned a corner; the gears grated as it accelerated out of sight.

Bannister wrote "Dear Stella." The words looked strange. He tore up the sheet of paper. "Dear Stella," he wrote again on a second sheet. There was no other way of starting. "Here I am in Tangier which is very nice. It is hot and sunny. There is a beach and the town is very interesting. I am staying in a nice hotel quite near to the beach. It is a long time since I wrote to you or heard from mother or you. How are you both? I hope that you are keeping well as I am. Mother is getting old I know but if she has good health it is not too bad. Health is the most important thing." The ball-point pen was running out of ink. He shook it and drew some circles on the blotting-paper. I have nice handwriting, he thought. The words looked neat but the writing was sloping a little. He moved the pad to another part of the bed and wondered what else he could write about. He had not seen Stella for at least twelve or thirteen years. It could be much longer, he thought.

"It must be twelve or thirteen years at least", he wrote, "since I saw you or mother. That is a long time. I suppose that mother would not recognize me now. Is her sight keeping good?"

He could hear Señora Perez banging noisily around downstairs. The rattle of saucepan lids and her voice raised in admonitions to the cat were a familiar part of every long evening.

"Does she still go to seanc . . ." he wrote. He looked doubtfully at the word before adding ". . . es?" It looked all right. I was always quite good at spelling, he thought, remembering the

170

boys shouting "Molly!", spittle shining on their teeth as they mocked him in a corner of the yard. Stella had been just as bad. He remembered being slapped by her in front of another girl, crying with vexation and shame as both of them had laughed at him and called him ugly names. He had tried to kick her on the shins but she had slapped him harder across the face and called him a little molly. She must have heard the name from some of the boys in the school.

"I often think", he wrote, "of when we were young. I wonder if you remember. We had some good times." He tried to remember something, anything pleasant but could not. It was all too vague. The room was unbearably stuffy. He went to the window and opened the shutters wider; the insects would come in but that could not be avoided. The talk with the Inspector had frightened him. He was getting at something, he thought. Some insinuation. He couldn't possibly suspect that I murdered Traynor. But you never knew with these foreigners. Their minds worked in different ways. They could not be trusted. They did not know right from wrong. He looked down at the street and the rusting bicycle frame and wished that he were somewhere else. It's time to move on, he thought, but the value of the monthly cheque was diminishing every year.

He went back to the bed and wrote, "I hope that your husband is keeping very well. I sometimes see his picture in the English papers. The cheque arrives every month from his solicitor. I appreciate it. Hasn't he done very well? The cheque is not worth as much as it used to be what with costs of everything going up but I manage all right." He would have to leave out that part about living in a nice hotel. This was not a time for being proud. Had Abu threatened him? Why shouldn't he tell the police about anything that he wanted? Why should he risk being involved? He wrote, "I do not know many people here," ashamed that this had to be admitted to someone who did not care. "My health is not too good." The letter, he knew, was full of contradictions. He would have to go back over it, rewrite it. "The climate does not suit me all that much. If I were in England . . ." He shook the ball-point pen and wondered how to continue. "I would be able to get. . ." He crossed this out and wrote, ". . . it would suit me better. Old friends and a better climate." She would know that this was not true; there were no old friends, no men in clubs asking "Whatever happened to old Bannister?", no woman looking back to their affair, no children, no one who cared. "It has been so long," he wrote. "It happened so long ago. The whole thing must be forgotten. When he hears about my health I wonder if your husband would reconsider the position. I am sure that I could find a job in London if I got back on my feet. That would save him money. The allowance would not be necessary or not the full amount anyway. I would like you to ask him, to put the position before him, of my health and that and se . . ."

He wanted a cigarette. He looked around the room to see where he had left the packet. It was on the floor. He lighted one and stood near the unmade bed. He could not post that letter. They would jeer at it and not bother to reply. I could go back, of course, but then the allowance . . . he thought. I could be murdered here. They murdered Traynor. An Englishman. If I had let him stay here last night. It would not have made any difference. Someone was after him. He coughed out the hot, harsh smoke and thought, If that policeman comes again I'll refuse to say anything at all. I'll demand a solicitor or a warrant. He can't come in here without a warrant. I'll have to rewrite the letter and post it. I can't stay here for the rest of my life. He sat on the edge of the bed and taking a new sheet of paper began to write slowly

"Dear Stella,

I know that both you and your husband will be sorry to hear that my health is not at all good. Mother also. I have seen a number of doctors but they have all told me the same thing. The many years that I have spent away from England have not at all been good for my health. All the doctors have told me that I must return to England as it is the only climate

172

where I can be sure of a good recovery. I am not complaining about having been away. I would not want you to think that. Both you and your husband have been generous to me and have done what you believed to be right. But at my age the sun is not good and there is no other country that would suit me except England. I am sure that you will understand and also your husband. It was my birthday the day before yesterday. I was forty-six, not as young as I was! We all move on. A close friend of mine was killed yesterday which came as a very great shock as you can imagine. He was an Englishman with a fine record as an officer during the war. I wonder if your husband knew him. His name was Traynor. I forget what regiment he was in."

Ash fell from his cigarette. He brushed it away and stubbed out the butt in the ashtray. It was a much better letter. He felt a sense of achievement. He should have written it before. It was better to lose one's pride than one's hope. They could not ignore it. He wrote, "You would have liked him. We lived in the same hotel and had many interests in common. My last visit to the doctor was only a few hours ago. He again insisted that I must return to England, so that is the position. Would you let me know what you think I should do and how the details could be worked out? The other business is so long ago that it must be forgotten." He tried to underline "forgotten", shaking the ball-point pen but there was no ink left. He would get another and finish the letter in the morning.

"So why you cry", Señora Perez asked, "if doctor tell you he is all right?"

"I was just upset, Señora. That other baby . . ."

"They do not care for baby here. You see them on streets, dirty and sick. You must see them there for yourself. They are not trained. No Christian think," she said. "I have a glass of Spanish wine for you." She took a tumbler from the table and filled it with dark, red wine. "You drink that," she said. "Good for sorrow."

"Aren't you going to have one too?"

"A little just because . . ."

She filled another glass. "Good for in here," she said, touching her stomach. "We hear that from saint. You prayed in our church for baby. Now look at him, healthy and sleep."

Johnny was asleep on a battered sofa beneath a picture of the Virgin.

"I met the Inspector."

"No good." Señora Perez shook her head emphatically. Some wine spilled from her glass on to her apron. She rubbed at it with her fingers and said, "Do not talk to him. He wants to make trouble. I tell you. He insulted me."

"But I hope they find out who killed Mr. Traynor."

"One of themselves, I know. Some savage from the streets. What do they care? They send their children after me like animals. Nothing at all."

"Why don't you go back to Spain, Señora?"

"To Spain?" The old woman looked at her angrily. "Why do you ask me such a thing? I own this house. No one can put me out."

"No," Janet said. "I'm sorry. I didn't mean that at all."

She wished that she had not come into the kitchen. She wanted to lie down and sleep if she could and not dream. "It's just that you're not happy here. You don't like the people," she said weakly. "Or the city."

"You do not mean me harm."

Señora Perez drank some wine and looked around the kitchen for her cat.

"Abdul," she said. "I called him Abdul. That was a mistake. He should have had good Spanish name."

"I don't want to keep you . . ."

"If I go back to Spain what will I tell to my sisters? Do you know that? Tell me that? Tell them that my husband went away with a pagan woman because I could not have a child? Do you think I should tell them that? What would they think of me then? I send letters to them every month.

I tell them that my husband is here. I tell them . . ." She hesitated and Janet wished again that she had not asked the question. She had preferred the image of Señora Perez; it had been as simple as one of her own beliefs. The old woman drank more wine and said, "I tell them I have three children. He forgives me." She pointed to a picture of Christ, bleeding, like a clown, upon a cross. "Two boys and a girl child I tell. I tell them their names and how good they were at school. All praised by the teacher. All of them. I tell them of the good jobs they have. Fine jobs in offices. And I tell them about the good boy who wants to marry my daughter Terese. How can I go back to Spain? And say it was not so? All the letters? All the years? Not so?"

"I'm sorry, Señora. It's none of my business. I shouldn't have pried," Janet said, remembering the Inspector's hand on her knee.

Señora Perez was a little drunk. She sat on a straight-backed chair, the tumbler held like a charm between her hands.

"So I must stay here," she said. "I cannot go back and let my sisters see the truth. They felt the envy. Envy? Is that right? The envy in their letters. They have said I am the lucky one. That the Virgin must love me. Their husbands are not rich men but they are good men. I know that my sisters are loved. When I heard", she said slowly, looking at the tumbler, "that I could not have a child. When the doctor tell me. After that I could not do that thing in the bed. I could not do it. My husband said I must. He made me do it some times but I could not do it again. It was never nice . . ."

"Señora Perez . . ."

"For you it is different. Not the same. You can have the babies. You can do it. But it was not nice for me. A priest said it was so. He told me that I was right not to do it. He said that I could offer it . . ." She finished the wine and brushed at the spot on her apron. "I cannot go home," she said. "You ask me. I told you."

"I shouldn't have asked you. I'm sorry."

"How would you know?" Señora Perez said without looking up. "You did not mean me harm. You could not know. I should not have written letters to my sisters. But He forgives me."

I mustn't cry now, Janet thought. She looked across at Johnny sleeping on the sofa. That's the second time today that babies . . . she thought. Or the third. Señora Perez was still brushing her apron.

"If there was anything I could do," Janet said, but she knew that there was not. The old woman was trapped by fantasy in the way that she had been trapped by David's trust. But the traps that one made for oneself were probably worse than anything that others could do.

Señora Perez said, "You will not tell any person?"

"No, I promise you. I won't breathe a word."

"I would not want anyone else to know."

"I promise, Señora. I give you my word."

Janet drank some wine. It was harsh and sickly sweet. I would help her if I could, she thought. The old woman seemed so helpless, sitting up straight in the chair. But what can you do for anyone except pretend that you understand and that you care? It was different with Johnny. He imposed his innocence upon her but she knew that he could change. He could be anything that she wanted him to be. Secure in her love he could make a life that was free from all deception. It was only in childhood that one had this chance. It could never return again. A sense of survival was fed to one like milk by someone who cared enough. She said, "The wine is nice," and heard Bannister come creaking down the stairs. "That's Mr. Bannister," she said, glad of the interruption.

"Huh!" Señora Perez shook her head. "That man. I will ask him to leave my house. He is no good. He bring the trouble on this house. Was he not a friend of that Mr. Traynor?" She stood up and put her tumbler on the table. "I will tell him soon to go," she said. "Without him or that Mr. Traynor there would be no trouble. There would be no police in this house."

176

She opened the kitchen door. Bannister was standing in the hall.

"Ah, Señora Perez," he said. "Good evening. I'm just going out for some dinner, you know. I don't suppose you'd have a ball-point pen. A blue one if you had it."

"What you say?" Señora Perez asked him loudly. "A pin? What you say pin?"

"A pen. Ah, Mrs. Merton. Good evening. I didn't see you there." Janet was surprised to hear him saying so much. He usually addressed her in a mumble. She said, "Mr. Bannister." He put his hat back on to his flat, bald head and said, "You may have heard me asking the Señora for a pen."

"I'm afraid that I haven't got one."

"Don't worry. I can get one somewhere tomorrow. It's merely an irritation." He was staring at her curiously. "You're all right?" he asked and she remembered that her face must be blotched and marked with tears.

"Yes, of course", she said, "I am," turning away from him, into the shadows of the kitchen.

"That's good," he said. "Then I'd better . . ." He started to move away towards the door. "A bite of dinner," he said. "I'll say good-evening to you both."

Señora Perez closed the kitchen door. "You hear," she said, "you hear? He is not a good man, that man. Without him no trouble. I must ask him to leave this house." They heard the front door open and Farrell's voice saying, "Hello."

"Don't let him come in here, Señora."

"Who? That Mr. Bannister? He gone. He say to have his dinner."

"No, Mr. Farrell."

"Mr. Farrell?"

"I don't want him to see that I've been crying. Please," she said as Señora Perez stared at her without understanding. "Please." Farrell knocked at the door.

"Are you in there, Señora Perez?"

The old woman looked blankly at Janet.

"In one minute, Mr. Farrell," she said. "I will come out.

Why", she whispered to Janet, "would you care? He is not a friend of yours."

"I just don't want . . ."

"I will not have more badness in my house. You have a little baby."

Janet turned away from her and heard her go to the door. "Yes, Mr. Farrell?"

"Señora, did Mrs. Merton come back?"

"Back?"

"You said she went to the doctor."

"No, she is not back."

"She isn't?" Janet noticed that he sounded quite concerned. She looked and saw that Señora Perez was speaking through the barely opened door.

"Shouldn't she be back by now?"

"How would I know that, Mr. Farrell?"

"I hope it doesn't mean that there's something wrong with her baby."

"If she prayed in our church the baby will be well."

"Yes, but all the same. A doctor . . ."

"I'm sorry, Mr. Farrell. Busy. Things that I must do."

"I won't keep you any longer, Señora. Thank you."

The old woman closed the door.

"Hah," she said, going to the sofa and looking down at Johnny.

"You wouldn't want someone to see you crying, Señora."

"I am an old woman, Mrs. Merton."

"I don't think you understand."

"I think I understand."

"You don't. There's nothing wrong."

"Too much wrong. Did not God give you a baby? Did he not save your baby when he was sick? Would you mock Him for that and spit at Him?"

"I'm not mocking anyone, Señora. I'm tired," she said, starting to cry again. "It's been such a terrible day. All the time. I'm so lonely."

"Lonely?" Señora Perez pointed to the picture of Christ on

178

the damp-stained wall. The daubs of red on his body might have been added by a child. No God should look like that. It made no sense; the bloody figure slumped drunkenly from the cross and the comic crown of thorns that only a fool would be given to wear. It was too unbelievable to be false.

Janet said, "I'll go to my room, Señora."

"I should not have told you those things. I should not."

"I've been upset. Worried about Johnny. Tired."

"You will laugh."

"How could I?" She picked up Johnny. He continued sleeping in her arms.

Señora Perez went to the window and opened a shutter.

"Abdul", she said, "should be back. He wanders from me now. If they get him . . . they tried to make fire from him before." She called, "Abdul! Abdul!" and from down the street a child's voice answered "Abdul!"

"I'll go to my room" Janet said.

The old woman stayed hunched and anxious at the window.

"I'm sorry if you blame me for something. I only didn't want . . . the tears," Janet said at the door. "I would be embarrassed. I thought. . . ." She closed the door and stood for a moment in the hall. She did not want Farrell to hear her. She climbed slowly up the creaking steps. He was certain to hear the sounds but he might think that it was the old woman looking for her cat. She went past Bannister's room and the cockroaches flat and glistening on the landing wall. She held Johnny tightly and climbed slowly to the next landing. Farrell was there.

He said, "You've been crying. Is Johnny . . . ?"

"The doctor said he was in perfect health. Perfect."

"That's very good news. I'm delighted to hear it," he said "I knew there was nothing wrong. But why are you crying?"

She opened the door of her room.

"Janet."

He caught her arm.

179

"Can't you leave me alone," she said. "I've had nothing but questions, questions. . . ."

"I want to talk to you."

"Not now."

"You're sure that Johnny . . . ?"

"Look at him."

"Then why are you crying?"

"Why is everyone asking me questions?"

"Who?"

"You. The policeman. Señora Perez."

"Oh you met the Inspector," he said.

"I met him."

"He upset you?"

"He thinks that we're sleeping together."

"That's quite a good idea," he said.

"And so does Señora Perez."

"Does she now?"

"I don't like being talked about," she said.

"Nor do I."

"Don't you? You don't seem upset about it."

He smiled. "I'll get over it," he said. "Won't you?"

She wondered what his smile meant as she went into the room and put Johnny lying on the cot.

"It's always so dusty in here," she said. "I just can't keep it clean. The other baby died."

"I'm sorry."

"Why are you sorry?" she asked. "You didn't father it, did you?"

"What on earth has that got to do with it?"

"Hasn't it? I didn't think it had but someone else did. Would you care if Johnny died?"

"Of course I would."

"Of course? Even though he's David's child."

"He's your child too."

"I suppose he is," she said. "But yesterday . . ."

"Yesterday's too long ago. Two days ago I hadn't even met you."

"And you know me now?"

"I'm not foolish enough to think that. But we've made some sort of start." He was standing in the doorway. "If you told me why you cried," he said. "I'd know you a great deal better."

She looked away and noticed a tattered cobweb hanging from the ceiling. All that effort, she thought, for nothing. And he wants me now. It's as simple as that for nearly everyone else. Not as a proof of anything. She said, "If you weren't here I'd cry for that spider. Does that tell you anything about me?"

He looked for the web.

"And if you weren't here," he said, "I'd probably decide to kill it."

"Maybe that's the difference."

"Maybe there isn't a difference."

"No please," she said, "not now" as he came into the room. "Not now with Johnny. Señora Perez . . . I'm sure she's listening to us."

"She doesn't own you, does she?"

"The way she spoke. It offends me that people won't leave me alone."

"What did the Inspector ask you?"

"All kinds of pointless things. Did I know Mr. Traynor? Did I know Mr. Bannister? Did Mr. Bannister know Mr. Traynor? It sounded like a parlour game. And he asked me if David might have gone away with Mr. Traynor. Why he thought that I can't imagine."

"They ask these questions."

"He asked you the same kinds of thing?"

"More or less the same."

"Too much has happened for one day," she said. "Two deaths."

"I heard that you went to the church."

"Señora Perez told me that I should. It seemed like a good idea at the time."

"You mustn't let her make too many decisions for you."

"I make my own," she said. "Why everyone assumed that just because David's away . . ."

She looked down at Johnny sleeping. "When I was a child," she said, "I don't think I ever slept as soundly as that."

"Can you come out to dinner this evening?"

"I don't want anything."

"But you've got to eat something."

"Not today."

"Janet," he said, "you're going to make yourself ill."

She sat on the side of the bed.

"It's a funny thing," she said. "I wonder why that policeman thought we were sleeping together. He said that someone heard you in here. But surely that isn't a proof of anything. People can be friends. They can talk. I'm not just something to be fucked."

She had expected him to be disconcerted but he was not. He said, "Maybe it wasn't an unreasonable suspicion."

"Did you ever see the prostitutes down near the market in the evening? When it's dark they carry pocket-torches," she said. "And they turn the beam on their faces so that men can see what they're like. Do you think that that's what being a woman is all about? Turning a light on your face?"

"Janet," he said, sitting beside her when she started to cry, "why don't you tell me what you want?"

"Could you give it to me?"

"Probably not but it's a help when somebody knows."

"I must look so ugly and stupid."

"You look neither, you look. . . ."

"There I go", she said, "putting the light on my face. Don't bother saying anything about it. I'd know it wasn't true and I'd hate you for telling me lies. Men tell such stupid lies, so much worse than the truth."

"I'll tell you the truth," he said, putting his arms around her.

"And you?" she said. "How about you? Do you think I'm just something . . . ?"

"No I don't," he said. "You make it sound so joyless."

182

"Isn't it?"

"Not always."

"Do you love anyone?" she asked. "And don't be stupid. I mean it."

"No. Do you?"

"Johnny. But of course you don't think that counts."

"I've changed my mind about that. And David?"

She pulled away from him and stood up.

"Yes," she said. "I love him I do of course."

"Love is never 'of course'. Anyway, I didn't say that you didn't."

"No, but you think. . . ."

"Don't tell me what I think," he said. "It's hard enough for me to know. And I won't try to tell you. Bargain?"

"Bargain."

She found a handkerchief and wiped her eyes.

She said, "I knew I was ugly. Like an old hag. I'll have to bring Johnny to the bathroom."

"For his bath," she added when he did not reply.

"Are you sure that you wouldn't like to come to dinner?"

"Certain. I have to do all kinds of things now . . ."

"I'll call in to see you when I come back."

"Do if you want to."

"I'll want to."

"I might be asleep," she said.

"But you want me to go now?"

"Not want to," she said, "but it's hardly practical is it? There's Johnny and Señora Perez. I'm sure that she's listening in the hall. She said . . ."

She did not expect him to kiss her. His tongue pressed between her teeth. She put her hands on his shoulders, and thought of David's routine that was always so predictable, even when he wanted her. She pushed him away and said, "Johnny . . ."

"All right," he said.

She did not say anything as he left the room. She saw her

face in the mirror. The tear-stains and blotched mascara reminded her of the blood on the picture downstairs. He had no right to trust me, she thought, going over to Johnny's cot.

# Chapter Seven

Lightning hissed across the bay as Farrell left the café. It lighted the roofs, the pointing minaret, the walls of the medina. They seemed to be blue against the dark green sky. The lightning hissed again and dogs howled dismally in some distant street. It was still uncomfortably warm. He threw away his cigarette and watched its red light flicker across the street towards a bicycle which someone had parked, its pedal caught on the pavement. The moths were everywhere. They brushed past his face; one hit him on the shoulder and fell to the pavement, its small eyes gleaming like the cigarette.

He walked towards Señora Perez's house. A policeman came from an alley but paid no attention to him; he stood there fiddling with a button on his uniform. I should have gone into the bar, Farrell thought, regretting what must have been cowardice. When the Inspector's car had gone he had waited, trying to make up his mind, wondering if it could be the same man, the same green shirt. No one else had come from the bar. He had watched the door for almost half an hour as if expecting someone he knew to come out and surprise him. Some women had passed, giggling when they saw him, walking gracefully, pots balanced on their shoulders. He should have gone in and ordered a drink and taken a look around but he had not done so. It had seemed sensible at the time. Now it looked like fear.

When he got to the house the door was locked. He saw a thin strip of light between the shutters of Janet's room. He knocked. Señora Perez's voice said, "Yes? What you want?"

"It's me, Señora. Farrell."

"Oh, you," she said dismissively. He heard her pulling back the rusty bolts. "I will keep it locked", she said, "every time from now."

"That seems wise."

She looked at him disapprovingly. Abdul came quickly down the stairs and went into the kitchen.

"Mr. Merton", she said, "will be back soon. Very soon."

"Has he been in touch with you?" She stared at him blankly. "Has he written to you?" he asked.

"No. No write, I just know. He said he would be back nearly now."

"Mrs. Merton will be glad," he said.

"Of course she will be glad. She love him. She is his wife."

"Señora, I don't think . . ." he said, then, changing his mind, "good-night, Señora."

"Good night."

She stood in the hall as he went up the stairs. It was not worth having an argument. He heard her closing the bolts on the front door as he passed by Bannister's room. She would listen but he did not care. He went to the bathroom and washed his hands and face in the tepid, rusty water. The floor was almost entirely covered by plaster that had fallen from the ceiling. The pieces cracked beneath his shoes like insects. He looked around for a towel but there was not one there. He dried his hands in his pockets and went to Janet's room. He knocked gently.

"You?" she said.

"Me."

"Hold on a minute," she said.

She was wearing a dressing-gown. He said, "You're lovely," and kissed her.

"You'd better shut the door and talk quietly," she said. "If Johnny wakes up . . ."

"Give him a sleeping pill."

"You'd make a great father."

"Do you really think so?" he asked. He saw that she was nervous.

"Janet . . ." he said. She interrupted him.

"Did Señora Perez say anything?"

"She said good-night."

"Nothing else?"

"It's the normal thing to say."

"Did you see the lightning?"

"Yes. I like it."

"Do you? It used to frighten me," she said, "but it's not like the lightning at home. It's usually over the sea."

"I should have brought you a drink."

"I have a bottle of wine."

"You're a genius. And a secret drinker."

"I sometimes get thirsty and I don't like to trust the water." She took a bottle from the wardrobe. "You open it," she said. "There's a corkscrew on the shelf."

She sat on the bed, her legs tucked beneath her. The long red dressing-gown was shapeless. He handed her a glass of wine and poured one for himself.

"You can sit on the chair," she said.

"That's a concession."

"Did you have a nice dinner?"

"Not really."

The chair creaked and tilted as he sat down.

"You're going to wake Johnny."

"He's a lovely child," Farrell said, "but he's also a bloody nuisance."

"I'm so sorry for the woman."

"In the café?"

"Yes. I keep on thinking about talking to her this morning. The way that she looked at me. She had real . . . dignity. Is that a silly thing to say? What do Muslims think happen when they die?"

"They go to heaven," he said. "They're buried very quickly. Mourners walk before the coffin. There's a beautiful passage in the Koran about the resurrection. You're not drinking your wine."

"Señora Perez gave me some earlier."

"Did she? That's more than she's ever given me."

187

She reminded him again of Catherine, of love turning into argument. She drank a little wine.

"Earlier this evening," she said, "when you were here, I said . . ."

"I remember, I said that I didn't think that you were."

"So what are you doing here?"

"It isn't the only thing. It's a part of things."

"That's vague."

"I wouldn't try to analyse it."

"Why not?"

"There are different levels," he said, and felt irritated by the talk.

There was no need to analyse a simple desire for someone else's body. Attempts at doing so invariably ended in the destruction of desire. It became too ridiculous. He said, "If it isn't simple it isn't worth it," and watched her push back hair from her forehead. "I always thought . . ." he said, remembering the later bitter fights with Catherine.

"You always thought what?"

"Nothing."

"You're cross."

"Not cross. How could I be cross? The simple fact is that we owe each other nothing. That seemed a good thing to me. If it doesn't to you . . ."

"Why should it seem like a good thing?"

"No scores to be settled," he said. "No points to be proved. No revenge. No resentment. No . . ."

"Love?"

"But it's love that brings all the complications."

"And most of the point, I would have thought."

"Some of it, not most. There's a very good point", he said, "in being purely and simply yourself."

"If that were possible. Do you believe that it is?"

"Not often. But it can happen."

"As long as there isn't any love?"

"That's a trick question. I just think that love makes it more difficult."

"So when people stop loving someone they became themselves again?"

"Not necessarily. They can. In a sense. It all depends."

She said, "I'm making you cross," and for a moment he wondered if she had been joking.

"It's not that I don't want to talk," he said. "I do. But not about reasons why."

"You know I love David?"

"If you say so."

"I wish that he hadn't gone away. That was selfish. Leaving me here with Johnny."

"Señora Perez said he'd be coming back soon."

"How does she know that?"

"She doesn't. It was meant as a warning. One begins to guess what happened to Señor Perez."

"No," she said, surprising him. "It's not something to joke about. The Inspector asked me . . ."

He saw, with a kind of relief, that she was starting to cry.

"I'm so sick of crying," she said. "I've done nothing else all day. I amn't like this. I think that people were staring at me on the street as if I were mad."

He sat down beside her on the bed. "What do you care?" he asked.

"I bet you despise me for crying."

"Why would I?"

"Well I do. I'm so sick of it. I don't know why I cry."

He put his arm around her. "It doesn't do any harm," he said.

"But it does. It makes me despise myself. It's a habit. I'll have to break it."

Her eyes seemed to be enlarged by the tears. "I don't want to wake Johnny," she said.

"There doesn't seem to be much chance of that."

I shouldn't be pleased, he thought, but he knew that the questions were over. She pressed close to him and he kissed her hair.

"I'm going to look ugly again"

"You'll never look ugly."

"You're going to start telling lies. The light on the face like I said."

Even when Catherine and he had been most in love he had noticed the triteness of their talk as if it were impossible to be even affectionate without reverting to aspects of childhood. One said predictable things, meaning some of them; there was safety in this routine. One sought reassurance, hoping that nothing would upset some inevitable pretence. One invented love names, private languages, creating someone new and simple and safe.

He said, "I want you," pushing her back gently on to the bed. She lay looking up at him, afraid, half-smiling, the tears still in her eyes.

"Do you?"

"Very much. You're beautiful," he said and looking down at her believed that she was. A tear ran along the side of her nose and caught on her lip. He bent and licked it away, running his tongue along her mouth.

"She said, "Forgive me if I amn't . . ."

He kissed her.

"You're forgiven," he said, "for nothing."

"You don't think I'm a whore?"

"Oh God!" he said. "Janet, could you really be so innocent?"

She tried to sit up but he stopped her.

"What do you mean?"

"Do you really not know?"

"I just asked a simple question."

"Then I'm sorry for snapping."

"But why did you snap?" she said.

"It's just that some of the things you say are . . . inappropriate."

"Inappropriate? I don't see how . . . ?"

"They lead to these kind of conversations," he said. "And these conversations lead nowhere."

"I'm sorry," she said resentfully. "I said that I wouldn't be . . ."

"Don't apologize. Why should you be sorry?"

Johnny turned in his cot and for a moment Farrell feared that he was going to wake. They both stayed still until they heard his breathing.

"It's Johnny being here," she said.

"Would you like to come upstairs?"

"But I couldn't leave him."

"Why not? I don't believe that's true. After all," he said, "you *leave* him when you're asleep."

"But I'd wake up if anything was wrong."

"Would you?" he asked to cover his irritation.

Farce was never too far away from sex; sometimes there was no difference. One might as well wear a false nose or fall on one's painted face.

"I would," she said seriously. "I'd know."

"Well he's fast asleep now."

"Do you really want me?" she asked. "It's not just . . ."

"I really want you."

"I want you," she said, turning her face away. "I didn't think that I would."

He kissed her cheek and put his hand inside the shapeless old dressing gown, stroking her breasts. "You're lovely," he said, wanting her, irritated that there was nothing else to say. The nipple beneath his fingers was long and hard. He took it between his teeth and she held his face in her hands, her fingers pressing hard into his ears. She said, "I'm sorry I was inappropriate." When he looked at her she was smiling. He sat up and took off his shirt. She touched his shoulder as if curious about its texture. Her fingers were warm. She stroked his arm and said "You're burned there. But you didn't get much sun," and he felt ashamed of his untanned body. "I'd prefer it," she said gently.

Although her face was still stained it was difficult to believe that she had cried; she seemed so resilient now. He stood up and took off his trousers; when he turned to her again she had opened the dressing-gown. She smiled when she saw that he wanted her. "You do," she said, as if it had been in doubt. She sat up and he felt the same old ache as if for Catherine's body. "Very much," he said. He helped her to take off the dressing-gown and put it on the floor. The shape of the bathing suit was marked in startling white around her body.

"That was Johnny," she said, pointing to a wrinkle on her stomach.

He kissed it. "It's nice."

"It might go away now," she said.

"I hope that it doesn't."

He put his arms around her, feeling her breasts pushing softly against him. They lay on their sides and Johnny moaned like an old man and turned restlessly in his cot.

"He's a good contraceptive," she whispered.

"Oh Jesus," he said, "in my trouser-pocket . . ."

"You don't need it. I keep prepared for David to come back."

"Clever," he said, kissing her. She pressed against him and the ache began to throb. He moved away a little, taking her breasts in his hands, stroking a nipple with his tongue until she gasped and said "It's too. . . ." He saw the marks of his teeth as she tried to pull him against her. They fought quietly with their tongues. He grasped and moved her roughly until the ache began to throb again. For a moment he feared that he had misjudged but it subsided. He defeated her tongue with his own, pressing it back into her mouth, holding it there until, unable to breathe, she ran her nails along his shoulder. He held her more tightly. She said, "Please . . ." but there was no fear in her eyes. She moved against him, increasing the strain of his desire. He moved his hand, his fingers pressing into the moistness. She kissed him, her tongue limp in her mouth and he became aware of his own breathing; the same rasping sound he had heard after following the man in the green shirt through the town. Her face was flushed, her forehead covered with tiny tears of sweat.

192

She seemed more beautiful, her eyes half-closed, her breathing as loud as his own. She said "Please . . ." and he moved on to her. He felt the caress of her fingers and feared that it would happen too soon. He pushed her fingers away and pressed slowly in through the moistness. He kissed her. "You want me," she said, tightening the grip of her thighs. "You want me." He moved very slowly and as the bed creaked he wondered if Johnny would wake. It would be typical; the red nose, the baggy trousers, the painted face. She rubbed the backs of his thighs with her feet. The sweat came down their faces like tears. Another minute, he thought, another minute, looking for some distraction, shifting his elbows slightly to ease his weight. He could think of no distraction. He kissed her, their teeth grinding, and it was Catherine, it was Janet, it was himself alone.

She held him very tightly. He stayed in her, stroking her, aware of a surprising tenderness that may have been guilt. She could know nothing of what he felt. He kissed her gently and she opened her eyes. He kissed her again, moving out of her. "Thank you," he whispered, feeling that he should apologize for things she knew nothing about. She shook her head and smiled and he noticed that there were tears welling in her eyes. He kissed them, the lashes pressing against his lips. She stroked his back. "I must have cut you," she said, looking at blood on her fingers.

"I'll live."

"And we didn't wake . . ."

"He's still asleep."

She looked across at the cot.

"I love him with all my heart," she said as if to reassure herself.

"He looks it."

"Does he?"

"Healthy."

"Not sick? I worried so much," she said. "I went to the church and prayed. If there is a God, He must think I'm such a horrid hypocrite. I know that *I* would. I hope that He doesn't exist. Does it worry you?"

"It used to. It doesn't any more."

"Why not?"

"It doesn't seem very important."

"I suppose it doesn't. It's just . . . I suppose it's what David says about superstition and that."

He felt a pang of jealousy. It surprised him. But of course she had a husband; someone to quote and talk about and betray.

He said, "I know it's conventional but I'd like a cigarette."

"I'll get them for you," she said. "Are they in your pocket?"

She got up, unselfconsciously and walked around the bed. The cover had left a pattern across her back, a web of faint red lines. He felt a stirring of desire again. It annoyed him. It was different now; it could not be simple any more. He watched her take the cigarette and a box of matches from his pocket. Her breasts swung heavily; the wide red nipples were like bruises. We could have married, he thought. Freedom is relative anyway. She should have had her baby. If I resented less. Grow up, she said. . . .

Janet sat on the bed and lighted two cigarettes.

"There's an ashtray," she said, pointing to the bedside table.

"I didn't know that you smoked."

"Only sometimes." She handed him the cigarette. "Would you like a drink?"

"Not now."

"If you don't want to talk," she said, "that suits me all right."

"But of course I want to," he said, pulling her nearer.

"Some men get so surly," she said.

"Have you slept with many?"

"Three or four," she said. "Have you slept with many girls?"

"About the same."

194

"Why did you ask me?"

"Curiosity."

"It's the first time I've been unfaithful to David."

"Is it?" he said. "He doesn't deserve you."

"Yes he does."

"No matter what we talk about," he said, "no matter what I say, you're going to find something wrong with it."

She looked towards the cot.

"If he woke up now," she whispered, "do you think he'd know?"

"How could he possibly?"

"It's the kind of thing you read about. A childhood memory that marks someone all their lives."

She moved away from him.

"Wouldn't that be an awful thing to do to a child?"

"Janet," he said, "you look after Johnny far too well. He won't thank you for it." She did not answer him. He had tried to keep the irritation from his voice but doubted that he had succeeded. A few minutes ago, he thought, I felt real tenderness for her. Or was it guilt? Or was it for someone else? He stubbed out his cigarette and watched a moth, crazed by the attraction of the lightbulb, fly around and around and around towards its death. The marks on Janet's back were fading. He sat up and kissed her shoulder. She said, "I know it's foolish," holding the cigarette awkwardly in her hand, the smoke streaming up past her breasts.

He smiled and said, "It isn't. You're very good to him."

"He's all I have," she said. "No. That isn't true. Sometimes I feel sorry for myself."

"Don't we all," he said, holding her wrist, stroking her fingers. She put out the cigarette. "I don't enjoy smoking all that much."

He pulled her gently down beside him. She looked at him trustfully. The tear marks were beautiful on her face. The trust disconcerted him; he had done nothing to gain it. He kissed her and felt her fingers move slowly along his thigh. "You're good to me," she said as he grew big in her hand.

"Doesn't David?" he risked asking.

"Not very often," she said. "Sometimes . . ."

She stopped and turned her face away from him as if some sense of loyalty made reticence essential.

They made love more slowly and gently than they had done before. The moth's shadow loomed and flickered like lightning above their heads. When he came in her she cried out as if hurt and he felt nothing for Catherine. It was like discovering that something one feared, that someone one had always hated would never again be a threat. He held her tightly. The sweat between their bodies dried slowly and they heard the moth fall heavily to the floor.

"You'd better go," she whispered. "Johnny . . ."

He kissed her.

"You can't be here in the morning. When he wakes up. We took such a risk."

"Was it worth it?" he asked, caring more than he would have thought possible about the answer.

"You know it was."

"For you too?"

"For me."

He got off the bed and felt suddenly foolish at being naked. He pulled on his trousers. When he turned, she had covered herself with the old red dressing-gown. He remembered her body so vividly that he felt jealousy stabbing like an old memory. He buttoned his shirt and they heard Bannister coughing.

"He must be just in," Janet whispered. "He'll walk around and cough for hours before he goes to bed."

"A most desirable neighbour."

"He gives me the creeps," she said. "Don't let him hear you leaving please. I don't want another lecture from Señora Perez. I hope the Inspector . . ."

"I'm sure we've seen the last of him," he said.

"He was so awful. Sitting there in his car. Asking personal questions. A big fat slug of a fellow. He put his hand. . . . I'm lucky he didn't try to rape me."

196

He picked up his shoes. "What did he do?" he asked and Johnny started to cry.

"Oh please. You know, I didn't want . . ." she said.

"It wasn't me who woke him."

"You should have whispered."

He wanted to defend himself but knew that it would be no good. She got off the bed, the dressing-gown fell to the floor. "Oh please . . ."

"Janet," he said.

She pulled it on.

"Please go when I ask you to. He mustn't see you here."

"He's only a baby."

"That isn't the point, is it? He's David's baby."

Johnny wailed with the kind of anguish that one would have thought could come only from experience. He gasped for breaths between each wail and Bannister coughed as if to register protest. Janet went to the cot. "Darling," she said. "What's wrong? Don't mind. Mammy's here." She picked him up and pressed his face against her breasts. "Please go, please go," she whispered.

"I'm sorry he woke up," Farrell said.

He left the room, closing the door as silently as possible. It was dark on the stairs. He went up, feeling the chipped wall with one hand, holding his shoes in the other. Johnny's wails followed him like bitter accusations. His hand brushed against some insect and a light went on unexpectedly in the hall; he heard Señora Perez coming noisily up the stairs. He opened the door of his room and feared for a moment that somebody might be there. He switched on the light. The room was empty. He closed the door and put his shoes on the bed. Johnny's cries were muffled now; less anguished.

He lighted a cigarette; he could hear Señora Perez speaking angrily in the room below. He opened his suitcase, took out some papers and read what he had written on the previous day; the description of the voyage from Gibraltar, the Atlas mountains and the first glimpse of Tangier, white and innocent in the sunlight. He tore them up and wrote on another page:

Dear Catherine,

Your letter, on thinking about it, seems quite fair. It was a cynical kind of invitation to extend but my motives were not consciously bad. I am not going to attempt analysis of myself or of you—we have done more than enough of that—but one or two things seem worth saying. I am inclined to take a lot of blame for the way things worked out. You are certainly more emotionally intelligent than I am and I was foolish not to recognize that. This isn't an attempt to get you back. I don't want that any more than you've made it clear you do. But I am sorry about the baby and for all that you had to go through. I know that I said it was simple but it could not have been. I've sometimes thought of it since —it was my baby too.

He heard Señora Perez going downstairs. Johnny was no longer crying. He wondered if he should go down again but decided against it; there were too many things that could go wrong. A cockroach crawled across the ceiling; he watched it avoid a crack and continue its journey. The Infant of Prague, stiff in the heavy frame, looked like a small boy dressed up for a party by his over-ambitious mother. It's a pointless letter, he thought, I won't post it. He wrote:

Perhaps we would have should have got married but that kind of commitment can't be forced.

If it hadn't been a trick—if we had decided on it together, it could have been different. But to make that decision yourself and to believe that it would make anything better. That was stupid. I'm glad the operation was . . .

He read back over what he had written and felt ashamed of it. He tore it up and added the pieces of paper to the others on the floor. They lay there, some words still visible—inclined, simple, stupid. . . .

He listened, hoping to hear some sound from her room. She must have gone to bed. She might even be asleep, he thought with regret. For a while she had seemed quite beautiful. The cockroach had reached the wall and had paused there as if uncertain of where to go next. But we still go on pretending, Farrell thought, that we know where we're going next and why we're going there because this pretence is what's supposed to make us human. If one refused to do so one was branded mad and ended up shouting on the street.

He switched off the light and opening the shutters looked out at the line of roofs. There was no lighting now. A sliver of moon made shadows in the sky. He could smell the heat; it came up from the silent street like a message from the damned.

# PART THREE

# Chapter One

She woke a little later than usual and heard the carts come creaking down the street. The room was almost bright; sunlight filtered in between the shutters. Her dressing-gown was on the floor. It lay there like a sleeping animal; the cord, twisted and trailing might have been a tail. She sat up quietly in the bed and saw that Johnny was still asleep. There were two glasses and a half-empty bottle of wine on the bedside table. It doesn't matter, she thought, staring at them. The label on the bottle was a brilliant blue. It doesn't matter; but she felt a little frighted as if about to face a stranger who would accuse her of some misdeed. She lay back cautiously and wondered what, if anything, had changed. The tick of the clock went on like the sound of the mules' hoofs coming from the street. I mustn't have set the alarm, she thought. It was a piece of evidence, a pattern broken, a departure from routine. Señora Perez must have seen the glasses. It's none of her business, she thought, trying to remember what had been said or a hint on the old and angry face.

She had a life of her own that was real and private. She should never have felt dependent. He could come back when he wanted to; she would feel affection. She might even love him again.

She could hear sounds from Farrell's room, the creak of a floorboard, the sound of the wardrobe being closed. When Traynor was there, she thought, who would have believed. . . . She regretted not having felt more sorry about his death. The death of Salim was different. One could understand it; the real violence was done to those who were left behind.

She thought about Farrell. He had been nice to her but she was not concerned about how he felt. She heard him opening the shutters. It was, of course, a pity that Johnny had started to cry. She looked at the cot with affection, remembering obscurely fragments of a dream. She had gone with David to see something strange in the hills. It had been in some kind of hut. Old men sat close to the entrance. The pedlar from the beach had beckoned them inside and pointed to the weeping statue of a woman. Other old men were kneeling around it. She remembered the tears and the old men's faces and from somewhere the hesitant voice of Traynor. David had laughed loudly, almost violently and she remembered that she had been ashamed at the way that the old men stared at him and his failure to understand.

She got out of bed, put on the dressing-gown and partially opened the shutters. The mules went past with panniers of oranges and lemons and branches of something green and all the vegetables that she had meant to taste some time. The Riff women walked like men. She watched them, bulky in their long dresses, disguised by their wide straw hats and thought that she'd like to see some mountain villages. Perhaps David would take her there. They could risk leaving Johnny alone with Señora Perez for the day.

She went over to the cot to wake him and saw that he was already awake. Fear came like a dream with all its unexpected logic; it rationalized old fears. She said, "Johnny" hardly daring to touch him. He stared up mercilessly at her, his eyes wide and expressionless, his face flushed and swollen. She picked him up and said "Little fellow. Was it something you ate or what? Darling, didn't the doctor tell me?" But he was drunk, she thought. No he wasn't. She said "I'll mind you. Don't worry. How long have you been awake?" He was breathing in a way that seemed normal but his temperature was high and his silence was worse than crying. Oh God, she thought, I'm sorry but you couldn't take it out on a little baby. David's laugh in the dream came back to her ears as if she had really heard it. "Please help me," she whispered to no one. "I'll get the doctor to come here," she said to Johnny. "He's good. He was good before when your tummy hurt." There couldn't be any connection. . . . She left him back in

204

the cot and started to pull on her clothes when somebody knocked on the door.

"Yes?"

"Just to say good-morning," Farrell said.

He saw her button her blouse. The dressing-gown was at her feet.

"You seem in a bit of a hurry."

"It's Johnny," she said.

"But isn't it always?" he said.

"He's really sick this time. I've just discovered . . . I overslept."

Farrell said, "He looks okay to me."

"Oh for God's sake," she said, "will you get Señora Perez?"

"Janet. . . ."

She said, "I'm sorry. I know. But it isn't that. I promise you it isn't." She put on her shoes. "I wanted to say something nice but I'm worried. He's really sick."

"Would you like me to get the doctor?"

She hesitated. "No. I'll get him myself," she said. "Señora Perez will stay here. It won't take long."

"It would be much more sensible for me to go."

"No," she said, "I don't want you to."

"Because he's David's child?"

"Not at all."

"What other reason then? Where does he live?"

"I want to go," she said loudly, fearing that she was going to cry. "He's my baby. I love him. Can't you understand? He might have seen you here last night."

"What in God's name has that got to do with it?"

"How would I know? Couldn't anything have to do with it? Do you know that it doesn't? I prayed for him, didn't I and he was all right then. Before we . . ."

"Janet," he said. "Sit down. You're going to make yourself ill if you go on like this."

"Don't tell me what to do! You keep on saying that I'm going to be ill. Do you think that I'm mad or something?

205

You've no right even to be here. Did I ask you to come in this morning? Things were all right before . . ." Her mind raced ahead of the words and although she was crying, she thought I shouldn't be acting like this. It's nobody's fault but my own. God, if he dies, I don't know. . . . She said, "Please tell Señora Perez."

"All right. If that's what you want."

"It is."

"But there isn't black magic," he said.

He left the room and she knelt beside the cot. "I'm sorry," she said, as if he were still there. "I know that there couldn't be any connection." Johnny had been well yesterday. There was something wrong today. It was probably something simple. A germ; the air was alive with germs. It was a wonder that something had not happened before. All this pointless crying, she thought, wiping her face with the back of her hand. "You'll be all right, won't you?" she asked as if she expected Johnny to answer. He continued to stare up blindly. His fists, she noticed, were clenched.

"Please Johnny . . ." she said as Señora Perez came noisily into the room.

"More badness."

She felt enraged by the singularity of the old woman's concern. But that's how I felt about Mr. Traynor's death, she thought.

"Please stay with him, Señora Perez. I'll get the doctor. It'll only take a short time."

"It's bad, I tell you, bad."

"It's just some kind of germ."

"God punishes our sins. The shame . . ."

She went out to the landing. Farrell was waiting there.

"Don't be foolish. Let me go," he said.

"No," she said, then added, deliberately, "We've done him enough harm already."

"Johnny?"

She was running down the stairs.

"And David," she shouted.

"Oh Christ!"

Señora Perez came from the room and blessed herself.

"Mr. Farrell. You will leave this house."

He did not answer her until he heard the sound of the hall door being closed.

"We have an agreement, Señora Perez," he said.

"You will leave this house, Mr. Farrell."

"I probably will," he said with a sense of relief. He could think of no reason for staying. One extricated oneself from complications simply by leaving. He had done it before.

He said, "Why do you want me to leave?" and followed her into the room. She stood beside Johnny's cot. He had no real interest in the answer. "Last night you were here," she said. "You broke a grace of God. You will not again in my house."

"I'll have to get my passport first," he said. "The Inspector has it."

"Ah the Inspector!" He was surprised by the sudden intensity of her anger. "Another such as you."

"You shouldn't make accusations, Señora. Charity . . ." he said, then stopped, ashamed of the hypocrisy. "Do you know where the police station is?"

"How would I know where? I do not know police! They never saw this my house before."

"I can always ask someone," he said.

"Grace," she said. The word seemed strangely pedantic. "Those who destroy it go down to hell."

"You mean a sacrament?"

"Yes, yes, a sacrament." She said the word with difficulty and he felt ashamed again. It was only too easy to mock her.

"I'll go to the police station now."

"You will leave this house."

"When I get my passport back," he said, going down the stairs. She shouted after him. "No! Today!" Four days are enough to have spent here anyway, he thought. He would leave without regret. He walked towards the centre of the town. The police station must be somewhere near there. She should have let me get the doctor, he thought, sorry that he was not with her. She was, in ways, too vulnerable to be coping by herself. But that was a problem for someone else; one became involved in other people's lives but it meant nothing. One's own future stretched on remorselessly ahead.

He walked down a narrow lane that looked as if it might be some sort of short cut. A sign above a doorway made him pause; a crudely painted silver bear. He went inside. The smell of marijuana pulled smoothly at his memory. They had smoked it in Catherine's flat, passing the cigarettes back and forth to each other, waiting for sights and sounds and ideas that were always disappointing. He was not surprised to see Susan.

"Well hello," she said. "It's you."

"I just happened to see the sign."

It was like an apology. He felt that he had stumbled on an old and private world that could never again be his.

"I was passing," he added.

"That's great."

He looked around the room, trying to identify shapes in the gloomy corners.

One shape laughed and moved.

"I was stoned last night," Susan said. "So I spent it here."

"Really?"

He felt impossibly old in his shirt and tie, with his Gibraltarian haircut.

"It's not much of a scene now," she said. "You must come back here tonight."

"I mightn't be here."

"Well, some othere evening."

"I meant that I mightn't be in Tangier. I could be leaving here today."

"Hey, that's not clever," she said. "You've only just got here." She swayed against him and he wondered if he should kiss her. One got into the habit. He said, "I just thought I'd move on," watching two shapes in a corner move together in what could have been a silent fight or the act of love.

208

"Then you're not going to meet Barrow."

"Is he not here now?" he asked her with relief. "That's a pity."

"You've just missed him," she said. "If you'd like to hang around. . . ."

"I'd better not." He tried to see his watch. "I've got some things to arrange. I don't suppose", he said, "you'd know where the police station is?"

"Telephone one nine," she said.

"You don't know the street?"

"I've no idea. Don't want to. Hey," she said, "aren't you deep! You aren't a cop, are you?"

He felt obscurely hurt.

"I'd know where the station was if I were."

"Maybe. All the same," she said. She swayed towards him again. He caught her by the shoulders and felt a twinge of desire waiting like a laugh that he was trying to hold back.

"What gave you that idea?" he asked her. "Have I flat feet or is it the haircut?"

She said, "I think I'll sit down." She sat on the floor.

"You wouldn't like a drink would you?"

"Jees!" she said.

He bent down beside her. The smell of marijuana came from her body as if it were a perfume she was wearing. She said, "All the same, you talked about Traynor and now . . ."

"Now what?"

"It's a coincidence?" she asked.

"Tell me what you're talking about."

"Ah come no now, don't mess . . ."

"Susan, I'd like to know about Traynor. I really don't . . ."

"Just a minute," she said. "He's the guy who was knifed. Right?"

"Two nights ago."

"Right. That's him. You know he was smuggling heroin down to Casablanca and Marrakesh and Rabat and Jees knows where?"

"How do you know this?"

"But everyone knows it. The swoop was on last night, wasn't it?"

"Was it? What swoop?"

"Come on!" Some buttons on her blouse were open. As she changed positions on the floor he could see in the near darkness the small shapes of her breasts. She sucked the tips of her fingers as if experimenting with some new taste then yawned and said, "Last night!"

He tried to remember her sitting hopefully in the boat with her tourist guide and her prim and fixed ideas. It had been a successful trip. She had got away from it all. The shapes in the corner started to move violently.

"Jees!" she said absently, looking at them. She could yet revert, Farrell knew, to the guides and the wistful hopes.

"What swoop?" he asked again.

"On the bar where the junk was. A bar down near the station. Some English guy owned it."

"Durcan?"

"Ah come on," she said. "Quit fooling. You know it all yourself."

"I happened to be there once. Accidentally."

She looked at him with disbelief.

"Well that's where it was," she said. "Durcan sold it. The fellows got it there. And your friend Traynor was a pusher. Only for the past few months . . ."

"That doesn't seem very likely."

"Okay. It was you who asked."

"Have you been taking heroin?"

"Are you mad? Did you never see a junkie? But pot is different. Did you know that it's less addictive than nicotine?"

"That's a quote," he said, "from 'Drugs on Five Dollars a Day'."

"Hey?"

"And they arrested some men?"

"Sure. Durcan was gone but they got four or five of the others. A friend," she said, "Robert, was just going down the street when he saw it happen. Was he lucky? Another minute and he'd have been in there. Did you ever hear about the prison in this town?"

"Run on the finest humanitarian lines?"

"Sure!"

"And why was Traynor killed?"

She shrugged her shoulders and seemed annoyed by the question. She looked towards the shapes in the corner. Someone laughed and Farrell wondered if it all had been a joke.

"How would I know?" she said. "I'll tell you though what Barrow . . . this fellow . . . thinks. He thinks that this Traynor was trying to keep the money for himself. Money that he got in the south. There'd be a lot involved. They didn't like that so they bumped him off."

The old Hollywood slang seemed so incongruous that he laughed at her.

"Okay," she said, "You asked."

She looked at him warily.

"You're remarkably well informed."

"Barrow knows what's going on."

"How's his writing going?"

"He's not writing at the moment."

"That happens," Farrell said, and wondered with a faint jealousy, if she had started to sleep with Barrow. Her innocence was going sour. She might never again be shocked by erotic dances in a club but she would still carry old attitudes around with her like a disease.

"I'm glad you're having such a good time," he said. She did not seem to hear him.

"He writes poetry as well as stories. His poetry is good," she said. "Have you ever read Creeley? He read me some last night. I could have wept at it. I really could."

He stood up.

"I might see you some time," he said.

"Sure," she said indifferently.

He went out, with relief, to the hot and narrow lane. The day seemed brighter. A dog growled softly. That's all I need,

he thought, a bite from a mad dog. He hesitated and watched
it dragging itself slowly along towards his legs. It paused and
growled again. He crossed to the other side of the lane, feeling
slightly ashamed as if he had failed some crucial test of nerve.
I could begin, he thought, to look like Bannister, shuffling
along in the heat and avoiding things. I wonder how well he
knew Traynor. He came to the end of the lane. The wide,
white street had the impact of a mirage. One almost forgot
that there were offices here and large department stores. He
asked an old man, "Police Station?"

"There."

A shaking finger pointed towards a building. Farrell
thanked him and walked towards it, wondering what to say
when he got there. He didn't even know the Inspector's
name. He would have to describe him. It could be a long, hot
session of incomprehension and frayed nerves. He crossed the
street and saw that the Inspector's car was drawing up at the
pavement. The Inspector beckoned to him. "A happy chance,
Mr. Farrell. I was just going to go to your house."

"A happy coincidence, Inspector. I was just going to go to
yours."

"Mine?"

"The station. It is, isn't it? Someone told me . . ."

"Oh yes. But you would not have found me there. I work
in another part of the city." He smiled. "Why were you looking for me?"

"I was hoping to get my passport."

"You are not thinking of leaving us?"

"It had occurred to me."

"That is a pity. I have it here."

He took the passport from his pocket and handed it through
the window.

"It's in perfect order," he said. "I was going to bring it to
you in case you might want it."

"Then I take it", Farrell said, "that I amn't a suspect any
more?"

"You never were one, Mr. Farrell."

212

"Wasn't I? You disappoint me."

"How could you have thought that?" The smile was framed by the window. "It was merely a simple check. A matter of routine. The woman in your house, that Spanish woman, should have kept a record of guests. I must have someone speak to her about it."

"She's a law to herself, Inspector."

"And that must not be encouraged, Mr. Farrell."

"I hear that Traynor was involved in smuggling drugs."

The Inspector stared at him impassively.

"Did you hear that, Mr. Farrell? What a peculiar story. Who could have told you that?"

"I don't seem to remember, Inspector."

"I'm not surprised, Mr. Farrell."

"Is it not true?"

"Not at all."

"That's odd. I heard that there was a raid on a bar last night."

"Was there?"

"As a matter of fact, Inspector, there's another coincidence. I just happened to see you coming out of that bar yesterday."

"Ah *that* bar," the Inspector said. He did not seem at all perturbed. "Some students with drugs. You know how it is, Mr. Farrell."

"There was a man with you," Farrell said. "He got into your car shortly after you left the bar. He was wearing a green shirt."

"Was he?" The Inspector took out cigarettes and offered one to Farrell. "I don't believe", he said, "that I see the point of your interest."

"I just thought that I recognized him," Farrell said. He refused the cigarette and felt the need for caution come as if he could see a warning on the Inspector's face or the fingers holding a match. "I could be wrong, of course," he said.

"Of course you could, Mr. Farrell. Who did you think that he was?"

"Someone who was in my room."

"In your room?"

"On the first night I was staying there. Someone searched the room. I surprised him but he hit me and got away."

"Did you report this incident, Mr. Farrell?"

"No."

"Why not?"

"I thought that I'd wait and see."

"See what?"

"See how things worked out," Farrell said.

The Inspector's lips made a small sucking sound on the cigarette.

"I'm not sure that I understand you."

"I could hardly have guessed . . ."

The Inspector got out of the car. He stood on the pavement, his leg holding the door open, his elbow resting on the roof.

"Do you wish to make a charge now, Mr. Farrell?"

"No."

"But this man. He attacked you, you say?"

"That's right. But I'm sure that he can't be found."

"Even though you believe that you saw him with me yesterday?"

"I saw someone who looked like him, Inspector."

"You're a cautious man, Mr. Farrell." The Inspector smiled and blew smoke through his nostrils as if he were performing some trick.

"Like you I have to be, Inspector."

"But of course, of course, I understand. Mrs. Merton. Such a very nice lady. Very nice."

The amusement on the round, fat face could hardly have been real. It seemed exaggerated, like the gestures and the slow, precise speech. Farrell tried to hide his resentment. "Mrs. Merton told me that she had spoken to you," he said.

"Such a very nice lady," the Inspector said. "But she was very overwrought about the death of some little baby. I cannot understand why any man would risk leaving her behind him. Mr. Merton must be a very innocent man. I look forward to meeting him soon."

214

They watched a bus go creaking past. Old women looked through the windows, their faces half-covered by yashmaks. The Inspector coughed and threw the cigarette away.

"So Traynor was not involved," Farrell said.

"Not at all, Mr. Farrell. Your information is not at all reliable. I hope that when you write news for your paper you check it more carefully. Mr. Traynor, as it happens, was attacked by two men in the medina. This kind of thing will happen. They were not men of this town. They were brothers who had come here looking for work. Mr. Traynor was homosexual. We have no objections to that. Who knows how it started? In defending himself . . ." the even voice went on as if the Inspector were teaching someone a language by constant repetition, ". . . shot one of the men. Not fatally, I am glad to say. He is now feeling much better. The brother of this man seems to have followed Mr. Traynor and stabbed him. That man is now under arrest." He smiled with satisfaction, rubbing his thumb across his chin. "Efficiency, Mr. Farrell."

"It seems very neat, Inspector."

"I try to make it that way."

The sun glinted off the smooth, black roof of the car. It was hot to the touch, Farrell noticed but the Inspector did not seem to mind. He leaned against it as if relaxing in a café. A single drop of sweat glistened on the side of his nose. He brushed it away and said, "I must not detain you much longer. There are, perhaps, things that you would like to see before you leave us. The mosque? Have you seen the mosque?"

It could be true, Farrell thought. It sounded plausible but it also seemed too neat. Detection was not a science; it moved through hints and triumphs and blunders towards a possible solution. Like a piece of reporting it attempted selection; one could never hope to know all of the facts.

"I've seen the minaret, of course."

"But of course. How could you miss it? It's really a beautiful building. Perhaps your cathedrals . . ."

It is just possible, Farrell thought, that the man in the

215

green shirt was a policeman. He remembered the way that Janet had smiled at his interest and felt a pang of regret. There was such innocence in every beginning; it always looked different from before. One wanted to believe in love. If he were a policeman, he thought, he would have searched my room because he was suspicious about Traynor then. He would do it secretly, not wanting to give a warning; they could have thought that I was some sort of accomplice. But the coats, I'd have known from the coats. . . . He looked across the Inspector's shoulder at the long, white street, the row of dusty trees, the cars, the cloaked men and women walking slowly along the wide, hot pavement.

"Do you, Mr. Farrell?"

"I'm sorry."

"Do you intend leaving on the steamer? The boat to Gibraltar?"

"No," he said as if he had come to the decision before. "Not if I can get a flight direct to London."

"You are near to an airline office here. You seem preoccupied, Mr. Farrell."

"Somewhat curious, Inspector."

"Really?" The smile flickered like a frown across the Inspector's face. "Why is that, Mr. Farrell?"

"I like neatness too, Inspector."

"Journalists do, Mr. Farrell. That's what makes so much of their work so facile. I think that I am using the right word?"

"Possibly. There are jagged edges."

"That is what I mean. As in life, Mr. Farrell, as in life." The smile returned and remained like a symbol of some victory.

"It occurs to me", Farrell said, "that my information may have been correct."

"I told you what I thought about that."

"No. You told me what I should think. And you told me *why* I should think it."

I would follow it up, he thought, if I was any good. But I

216

won't. Because anything I do is bound to involve Janet. He'd make certain of that. I'm sure that he's implicated, that he gave the warning to Durcan to get away. That's what he was doing in the bar. And Traynor may or may not have been involved. There's a story here if I worked at it. But is it worth more suffering to someone, interrogation, the end of her marriage perhaps? Cummins would say that it is. I don't think so.

"There is a missing link," Farrell said. "It doesn't feel right to me."

The Inspector laughed and got back into his car.

"Really, Mr. Farrell," he said. "You disappoint me. I thought you were a serious man. Now you sound like some cheap *roman*."

"It's not my kind of story," Farrell said. "We can always get it from the agencies."

And he may be telling the truth, he thought defensively.

"That is nice for your readers, Mr. Farrell." The Inspector smiled and started the engine of the car. "I hope that they enjoy reading about Morocco", he said, "and come here to see for themselves."

"And be murdered in the medina."

"I'm sure that the trial will produce some simple facts."

"If you have anything to do with it, Inspector, it will."

The Inspector put the car into gear. "I am sure, Mr. Farrell, that I will meet you again. Next year, perhaps. Although I know London I have never been in Dublin. I may yet go. But it is more probable that you will come back to Tangier. Is Mrs. Merton returning to Dublin soon?"

"I didn't ask her."

"It is so nice to meet old friends."

Farrell watched the car move away. What does it matter, he thought, a couple of inches on the first or third page of the paper. One shouldn't attempt to reduce people's lives and deaths to such a derisive shape. To give them so easily digested a neatness was to falsify all that they had been.

He walked slowly along the pavement and stopped outside the airline office. The gaudy posters in the window seemed to hold some sort of reality. PARIS MILAN LONDON NEW YORK. He went inside.

# Chapter Two

When Janet got back, Señora Perez was kneeling near Johnny's cot. She looked forlorn and untidy as if she had not had the energy to move. The tired words of her prayers came like the whispered words from a confessional. She did not look up. The light in the room was dim; the shutters were closed and the air was heavy with heat.

Janet stood in the doorway and said, "He isn't worse?", feeling reluctant to look. The stare had seemed so reproachful, the eyes of someone who felt that they had been betrayed. She went to the cot and saw that Johnny was sleeping, his fists still tightly clenched. The fever may have eased slightly; his face did not seem so flushed.

"No worse," Señora Perez said. She stayed there huddled on her knees. "No better. My prayers have not been heard. Where is doctor?"

"I came ahead of him. He said he'd get here as soon as he possibly could."

"Ah." The old woman expressed her doubt. "You should pray here with me now."

"No! He's not a corpse."

Señora Perez blessed herself, and thumped her chest.

"Please don't kneel there, Señora. It can't do any good."

"No good? No good in the prayers?"

"I don't mean that." She wanted to hold Johnny in her arms but could not risk waking him. "I mean just now. It doesn't help me," she said.

"You must learn much, Mrs. Merton."

"Please Señora."

"To be like little child."

"God must love children all right," she said bitterly. In moments of hate one believed in Him. One had to believe

219

that there was some ultimate plan. He forced one to belief through hate, to recognize that somewhere there must be a pattern that rationalized all the suffering and sadness and inequality.

"He takes them for angels to Himself."

"Well He won't have mine," she shouted. "I minded him every second of the day. You know that. I never left him alone. I'm sorry," she said, feeling defeated and foolish.

"You must send for the priest, Mrs. Merton. I blessed him with holy water myself."

"He's not going to die, Señora. An injection. . . ." She tried to speak as reasonably as she could. "The doctor will be here in a moment." It was like coming face to face with her own worst fears; the old woman might have been her mother. "It must have been a chill he caught," she said, "A draught. The change in temperature."

The doctor had been defensive as he had stood listening to her in his doorway. "There was nothing wrong yesterday," he had said. "I examined him thoroughly." She had noticed several new blood-stains caked under his chin. "I'll come up and look at him. Storm in a tea-cup perhaps."

"Please don't kneel there," she said.

Señora Perez stood up, swaying slightly, as if about to lose balance. She brushed the front of her apron and said, "All of us are punished." Her hair had escaped from its bun.

"It's not like that," Janet said. "If Jesus were any good why would He let . . . ?"

"Good? He is all good."

"He couldn't love . . ."

"The real love."

"Please go away, Señora." She felt too tired to be angry. "I want to be with my baby."

"Huh, do you hear those savages?" Señora Perez said. Children were shouting in the street. "And Abdul he is not here."

The mocking, raucous voices went on like some ancient, ritualized chant.

"Marks and Spencers. Hey, Charlie Chaplin. Charlie!"

"They will kill my Abdul if he is there."

Janet opened the shutters. "That's strange," she said. "Why would they mock a pilgrim? I thought they respected their holy men."

"Holy!"

The children were following a tall man dressed in a shabby brown cloak. He came down the street, ignoring them, holding a staff in his hand.

"Where the horse, Tom Mix?"

"They shouldn't!" Janet said. The man's head was bowed, his beard spread across his chest. It was not until he had stopped outside the house that she recognized him.

"Señora," she said, "it's David."

The children gathered around him. They seemed suddenly nervous. He said something to them and they laughed.

"Superman!"

"I tell you," Señora Perez said. "I tell you he come back."

"Please go down, Señora. I don't want you to be here. And let *me* tell him about Johnny."

He was giving the children money. She could see the top of his head, his hand clenched on the staff. The children scrabbled for the coins that had fallen on the pavement. Why would he make such a fool of himself, she wondered. "Go down, Señora, please."

"I go."

She heard him coming into the hall and Señora Perez raising her voice in greeting. She looked at herself in the mirror. Oh God, she thought, why now. Why now and why is he dressed like that? He had laughed in the dream, foolishly. She had felt bitterly ashamed; the glasses on the bedside table, the tousled, unmade bed and Johnny unwell, the spider's glistening web. She looked around for her lipstick but could not find it. The doctor should be here soon. An injection, she thought and then we can go. . . . David's staff tapped against the stairs. She did not turn as he came into the room.

"Well," he said. "It's me. How have you been keeping?"

She turned around slowly.

"All right."

He was smiling at her.

"How are you?"

"Great!"

"You look awful."

"The gear? It's practical," he said. He put his staff on the floor. "How is Johnny?"

"He's not well."

"Not well? What's wrong with him then?" He looked down at the baby. "It's nothing serious, is it?"

"I don't know. How would I? I've sent for the doctor," she said. "You left us so long . . ."

"Now hold on a minute, Jan."

"You haven't even kissed me."

He kissed her predictably and calmly. "What on earth's the matter with you?" he asked.

"Your beard . . ." she said.

"Never mind the beard."

"Another child died," she said, resenting his calmness. "I was afraid that Johnny . . ."

"What doctor are you getting?"

"The one that I went to before."

"You should have gone to the hospital," he said. "The Spanish Hospital here is very good. Did Señora Perez not tell you?"

The old woman came bustling into the room as if she had been listening at the door.

"You know the Spanish Hospital, Señora?"

"Yes, Mr. Merton."

"I must go and 'phone them."

"Very good Spanish Hospital, Mr. Merton."

"Then why didn't you tell me about it?" Janet said angrily.

"Hold on a minute, Jan."

"You say your own doctor," Señora Perez said. "Nothing but trouble here, Mr. Merton. Mr. Traynor was killed."

"Was he really?"

"We had police in the house." She looked dismissively at Janet. "And other bad things happening. Why are you dressed like pagan, Mr. Merton?"

"Never mind about that, Señora."

"You look like a bloody fool," Janet said, wanting to hurt him. "All the children were laughing at you." For a moment she was tempted to tell him that she had slept with Farrell. Maybe that would shake his calmness. His face was so heavily bearded that she could not detect his expression. But if he found out he'd probably leave me, she thought. He might be glad at the chance. "I'm sorry," she lied. "It's different now that you're here. It was so lonely. Did you miss me?"

"Of course I did."

"I'm worried, Mr. Merton."

"Señora?"

"My cat Abdul has gone."

"Oh for God's sake," Janet said. "What about my baby?"

She took Johnny into her arms and kissed him. He winced up at her and started to cry.

"That sounds healthy enough," David said, as if he were talking about something that only remotely concerned him.

"I am afraid that those bad children have killed him."

"They won't do that, Señora. Cats are respected here. The prophet cut off a piece of his robe rather than wake one that was sleeping on it."

"Why doesn't that doctor come?" Janet said. "That's a bloody silly story."

"It may be to you. Frankly, Jan, I think you're just making a fuss. There's obviously nothing wrong with him. Give him to me."

"Don't touch him with those filthy clothes."

"All right," he said in a tone that he always used when he humoured her. "All right."

Señora Perez said, "I don't know," and went out, leaving the door open.

"You shouldn't have snapped at her", David said, "when she's worried."

"And what about me when I'm worried?"

"It's all going to work out. Don't worry."

"Oh of course it will," she said bitterly, holding Johnny tightly in her arms. He had stopped crying and seemed content.

"Please take me away from here, David. I hate it."

"I was planning to," he said.

"To Paris?"

"Not yet. To Rabat."

"No, I'm not going there," she said.

"Look, we'll talk about it later."

"No!"

They heard someone coming into the house.

"Maybe that's your doctor now," he said.

"I'm going back to Dublin. I don't care . . ."

"Later, Jan, later."

Farrell stopped in the doorway and said, "Hello, did the doctor come?" He stared curiously at David.

"This is my husband," Janet said, feeling ashamed. He must be laughing inwardly at that ridiculous cloak and the unkempt beard.

"My name's Farrell."

She watched them shake hands and listened to their attempt at conversation. She did not know either of them and neither of them, she thought angrily, know me. Any man could invent her in any way that pleased him; then she would live on his mind, a falsification that happened to suit a mood or a need. She felt so alone that she feared that she would cry again. Please, she thought, please, oh please. She heard Farrell say that he was going to London. She nodded when he said goodbye. She did not care. I'm a special person, she thought. I amn't just what I need. I must believe in something and start to know. I mustn't invent myself. She saw that David was staring at her. Johnny was quiet in her arms.

# Chapter Three

Bannister sat at the café table. The cheap new ball-point pen had started to leak. The ink was staining his fingers. He rubbed them on the side of the chair and wondered if Abu would come. He was determined to tackle him about the Traynor business. He looked at the sheet of paper. It still isn't right, he thought. They would see the panic in the words.

"After that business with the cheques I know that your husband was embarrassed to be related to me. He explained that being in politics he could not afford a scandal. It was good of him to give me the allowance but it was all so long ago, surely he does not think that it would happen again!!! A man is entitled to his mistakes. If I could have the allowance in England I could settle down in Brighton or somewhere like that. Blood is thicker than water, Stella, and mother is not as young as she was. As her only son . . ."

He wanted a drink. The waiter had gone inside. If Abu turns up, he thought, I'll settle this Traynor business for once and for all. I could get married in England. Live in some nice little house. Sweat trickled across his forehead and came down along his nose. Some woman who appreciated . . .
"It's you, Mr. Bannister."
Farrell was carrying a suitcase.
"Would you like to join me?"
"No, thanks. I'm hurrying off. I've got to catch a plane."
"Oh you're going," Bannister said with a sharp envy. He rubbed the sweat from his nose. "I didn't know. Going south?"
"No. A flight to England."
"That's nice for you," Bannister said. He stared at the top of the table, the sheet of paper, some ink stains, his dusty hat.

"It's a better climate," he said. "We British, if you don't mind my saying so, we know how to live."

"There's just one thing," Farrell said. "When you get back to the house, if Abdul isn't there. That's the name of the cat, isn't it? I'm afraid he's dead. At least there's one just like him lying at the end of the street. There's wire around his neck. I'd have brought him back if I weren't rushing for the plane."

"I never liked that animal," Bannister said. "It struck me as very sly."

"She's going to be upset. It's been very nice knowing you, Mr. Bannister."

"Good-bye, Mr. Farrell."

He looked at the dusty hat, the stains, the letter that he would never post. Where was that bloody waiter? "Waiter!" he called but, as he expected, nobody responded. "Waiter!"

The thing about health is the best, he thought. They can't argue about that. Anyway it's true. I don't feel at all well. A man can get tired and run down away from hearth and home. These foreign countries. . . .

"Hello there, Charlie Chaplin!"

He looked up slowly. The boy was not smiling. He was wearing the same yellow tee-shirt. He had left his box on the pavement.

"Now you pay me right, Charlie."

"If Abu catches you here again."

"He gone to prison, Charlie. Now you pay me fast."

"Prison?" Bannister said.

He searched one pocket. "I'm short of change."

The boy tapped him on the knee.

"Fast, Charlie."

He felt afraid.

As he searched in his pockets he looked away towards the bay and the glistening stretch of sea and a distant foreign country called England.